ELENA SOBOL

EMERGENCY UNDERWORLD

Copyright © 2023 by Elena Sobol

All rights reserved.

No portion of this book may be reproduced in any form without written permission from the publisher or author, except as permitted by U.S. copyright law.

Edit: www.copybykath.com

Cover Art: https://coversbychristian.com/

1

NOT ALL ROADS TO Hell are paved with good intentions. Some are just paved, which is good for my tire tread. I jerked the wheel as the van shot up from the Gates of Hell and back to the human world. My stomach wobbled. It would take days to wash the reek of sulfur out of my hair.

The traffic flow of Reno barely registered an EMT van that appeared out of nowhere. I rolled down the window. The stench of burning flesh wafted out into the fresh air. Hell is a disgusting place, which is saying something. I've been a soul rescuer for six years and have seen my share of Underworlds. The first time I'd gone down, I'd donated my breakfast burrito right on top of my old partner's shoes. That probably explained why no one wanted to ride the van with me, except for Rudy. Well, that and the fact that I was a dragon shifter and ate literal human souls.

"Why do Abrahamic religions put their dead in that place?" Rudy asked. He was using first-aid gauze to rub demon blood off his hand blades. We had to break up a nest of devourers, the demons of gluttony, to get to our rescue this morning. Really, we should've backed off and called the main office. Except that would've meant losing our guy.

I raised an eyebrow at my partner.

"General masochism?" I wiggled my fingers. "Fire and brimstone, watch out!"

Rudy humphed. He looked entirely too at ease in his human skin. Long, muscular legs strained his leather pants and the lines of his face sketched a pretty surfer boy. Wavy blond hair completed the look. I was the one of the few people who could see the skull that gleamed under his skin. Rudy is reaper royalty. He's as good with his ulaks as freaking Riddick and tracks souls like they're deer. Compared to him, I'm a punk ass kid who trips over her own shoes. He's my lookout while we're in Hell, Mag Mell, Hades, Duat or whatever Underworld we're rescuing souls from. Why he'd chosen me for a partner was beyond me, but I don't look a gift unicorn in the teeth. Plus, that he chose me really pisses off the valkyries. A win's a win.

And me? I drive the van. Mostly.

One nice thing about our ridiculously overpowered van is the multitude of important first aid features. Like keeping my Red Bulls cold. I pulled the can out of the refrigerated cup holder and took a sip. The headache I'd felt the last few hours finally retreated into the depth of my brain. Probably to fester as mental illness.

"I honestly thought you were from there," I said.

"I'm from Purgatory, like all the reapers," he said. "Your ignorance is truly extraordinary, Chrysoberyl."

I wrinkled my nose at his use of my full name. "Like you know where I'm from."

He paused before starting on the second blade. "You're from Vyraj, like all the Slavic demigoddesses."

"Nope!" I said brightly. "I'm from Tempe, Ari-zow-na."

Grinning at his scowl, I turned onto North Virginia street. Supernaturals counted their parentage as their true origin and not the place of their physical birth. That was fine. I might've been born in a no-name hospital in Arizona twenty-seven years ago, but I grew up in a van. By American standards, I was "from everywhere, you know?" Thank my nomadic mom for that. She was also to thank for naming me Chrysoberyl Green, which I'd shortened it to "Chrys." At least she didn't name me "Diamond." I'd make a terrible stripper.

Casinos rose on either side of us as we followed the road to the Reno Arch: Silver Legacy and Eldorado. The ERS headquarters was located in the center of the city. Out of habit, I read the sign as it rolled over our heads. "Reno, The Biggest Little City in the World." I turned toward Reno City Hall. The glistening black building housed the Emergency Rescue Services in its underground tunnels. The stone in my bracelet clinked off the steering wheel. It had turned from a blue to a pulsing amber. My dragon wanted out. I gritted my teeth and stepped on the gas pedal.

We burst onto the plaza and the magic of the ERS headquarters made stone and metal part before us. I slowed before the Space Whale statue. It pictured a full-scale mother whale and her cub, and was one of many Burning Man art pieces dotting the city. The festival attracted both the incense-loving nomads like my mom and the crunchy granola folk. The multi-colored glass made the asphalt beneath it radiate with color. Pausing on the glowing platform which can only be seen by ERS operatives, I killed the engine. I tapped my nails on the steering wheel.

"Easy, Green," Rudy said, his eyes on my bracelet. "You've got time."

I nodded. He'd never really seen me "dragon out", but telling him about my soul-devouring form had been a sensible precaution. Not that he wouldn't have heard the rumors. Finally, the platform wobbled and dropped us into the bowels of the city.

The ERS headquarters burrowed into the Reno underground like a monstrous naked mole rat. We were a branch of the Spiral, the inter-dimensional police that managed the supernatural communities. And monsters, there were always monsters. Thanks to its location in the universe, Reno was overrun with them. At least they kept freaks like me employed. Silver linings.

When we finally stopped moving, I slid out of the driver seat and jogged around the back of the van. As the lights blazed on at the reception platform, I swung open the barn doors.

Inside was a glowing shape that vaguely resembled a man. He hadn't been in Hell very long, and the demons had only nibbled on bits of his matter before Rudy and I showed up with guns—and ulaks—blazing. Now, he sat in handcuffs that hummed around his wrists with embedded wards. The van's magical seals buzzed around us like electric fly traps. At the sight of me, he flinched back like I had horns growing out of my head. That was just rude, since I didn't have horns. At the moment.

I folded my arms over my chest and stared him down.

"Come on, Tony," I said. "Don't be shy now."

I make at least five rescues a week. Six, around full moon. Humans get themselves kidnapped by monsters all the time. Sometimes, it's their own fault—like using a Ouija board on Samhain. Other times, it's an accident like stumbling into Faery on a hiking trip. But no one, and I mean, *no one* deserves to be kidnapped more than summoners.

I thought back to his file. Tony Alvarez, 32, a software tester by day, a demon summoner by night. He'd tried to summon Beelzebub by drawing his seal on the floor of his mother's basement.

"I'm not going," he mewed.

"Summoners," Rudy murmured from behind me. "They're all dumb as Freud. We should've just left him."

I stopped myself from agreeing with him. Sure, Tony wasn't the sharpest knife in the drawer. He was lucky he'd botched the summoning seal and only attracted devourers. If he'd managed to summon the actual Beelzebub, he'd be nothing but a bloody stain. As it was, the devourers grabbed his soul and dragged him to Hell like an unsanctioned power snack. Tony's mother had found his comatose body and called 911. She was crying over him now, no doubt. Her tear-stricken face was the reason I'd braved the devourers that morning. I knew what it was like to have a mother who had to deal with the aftermath of her child summoning a demon. Of course, I'd been *twelve*.

"You'll throw me in the dungeons," he said. "I know the Spiral's laws." So, he knew better and drew that circle anyway. The wards pulsed around him as they responded to his angst. The dragon inside me whined as my bracelet thrashed against my wrist. Demons could fuel themselves for days using human souls. Especially if they were trespassing in the human world. And me? I could slurp this little fool up like a milkshake.

I shuddered. "Better than being soul-dead. Trust me." I turned to Rudy. "Call the selkies."

Rudy gave a sharp, low whistle, and I heard footsteps coming from the bowels of the building.

Tony shook his head and tried to make himself small.

"No, no," he whined. "Please."

I could see his essence shedding. His soul had been separated from his body for too long. Five more minutes and Tony's mother would be crying over a corpse.

Closing my eyes, I reached for the dragon within. I could feel my horns pierce the hair at the top of my skull and scales bristle under my ERS uniform. I sang in Old Slav, the language of my father.

"Small goat, little goat, come to my stead. Not where, not there, but here instead." The song uncoiled inside of me, and I suppressed the dragon. She strained against my skin. *"I will groom you, I will feed you, tie you to*

a stake. Come to me, to my stead, not there but here instead."

This was a shepherd's song, one of many I'd heard when visiting the Slavic pantheon. For some reason, they were the ones that had stuck with me. It wasn't the meaning of the words, but the intent behind them.

His eyes widened as his form drifted toward me. My dragon was a predator, but housing her had perks. Like being able to summon souls.

A pair of twenty-something brunettes shouldered me out of the way. They had brought a stretcher with them. The selkies, Anne and her brother, Henry, were Heal Hands. The supernatural equivalent of a paramedic. Only with a lot more knowledge on magical poisons. I kept singing as they tied the now-unresisting Tony down.

Henry winked at me. "Alright, Chrys?"

His sister threw him a seething look. I wasn't popular with the healers, but Henry seemed to be the exception. I was probably my personality and *not* my sculpted ass. I returned the wink.

"Oh, you know, another day in Hell."

As they sped Tony toward the resuscitation wing, I chugged my Red Bull. The sides of the van were still a little sooty after we busted out of the Gates of Hell. The ERS symbol looked similar enough to the human EMT's Star of Life to be overlooked if accidentally glimpsed by mortal eyes. The primary difference is that instead of the staff of Asclepius, the middle of the symbol pictures the Orphic egg. The serpent curling around it is Ananke, the World Eater. Also, it's gold. A tribute to the Spiral's golden ammonite.

I crushed the can and cast a nervous glance at my wrist.

"Go," Rudy said. "I'll restock and park her."

I nodded my thanks and wobbled down the hall.

The ERS station lay in one of the old tunnels that ran under Reno. It had all the charm you'd expect from a subterranean concrete labyrinth, but at least there was coffee. Itching in my scales, I walked past the bunk beds. A couple of them were occupied—I recognized a witch from day shift and a vampire from the night. The latter gave me a sharp-toothed grin and went back to his pack of fake blood. I nodded and hurried past. Last thing I wanted to do was engage in small talk. With so many kidnappings happening every day, there was little time for gossip around the water cooler. Not that people were usually interested in chatting with me.

My father is Veles, the god of the Slavic Underworld. The Great Dragon that dwells in the roots of the World Tree. His horned visage puts fear and awe into men's hearts. He is famous for being fierce yet fair. The god of cattle and magic. Unfortunately, that reverence doesn't extend to his daughter. Don't get me wrong, I don't have daddy issues. I met Veles when I went to connect with the Slavic pantheon at fifteen. Every demigoddess needs to claim her god power to have full access to that supernatural tap. Usually it was something cool, like power over thunder and lightning, or just the good old super strength. When my power came to me fully, I got my dragon.

I walked past the lounging area that was dotted with couches and breathed in the sour smell of stale coffee. The lockers and the pool were up ahead. This was my chance to let her out, even for a few minutes.

Kicking off my Doc Martins—great in combat, bad for swimming—I shoved the door open with my shoulder. Inside, chlorine replaced the smell of coffee. I began shuffling out of my clothes as I walked toward the glistening water of the Olympic-sized pool.

I pulled my ERS shirt over my head and kicked off my quickly shrinking jeans. I barely made it to the water in time. The dragon bursting out of my skin, I dove beneath the surface.

2

AS FAR AS THE scaly lizards ago, I'm not a very big one. My length barely breaks twenty feet. Most of that is my neck, and most of my dragon form is transparent. I am partially incorporeal. My short legs and a wingless back make me more of a wyrm than a proper dragon. Back when I was seventeen, my mom took me to the Spiral's expert on the supernatural species. He had prodded me with devices and fed me bitter-tasting poultices. It was a mystery to him why my dragon appeared in a ghostly shimmer but felt solid to the touch. Outside of the questionable usefulness of being nearly invisible underwater, he couldn't find any practical use for it. This was years before I knew she craved souls.

Relief washed over me as my dragon stretched her form into the water. Luminescent coils glowed silver-blue under the surface. My human self was gone and my shifter form luxuriated in the cool water of the Spiral's pool. Lake Tahoe would've been better, of course. I remembered the summers I'd spent swimming in the depths of the turquoise lake. Just thinking about it made me itch. The brown sugar sand and the rippling waves carried by the mountain winds? Pure bliss.

I shoved the craving aside. The pool would have to be enough. Here, within the walls of the most powerful agency in the supernatural world, the chances of my dragon lashing out were small. The glass roof above had been opened for the warm season. Sky spilled sunlight down to the tiled bottom of the pool. Underworlds weren't exactly rich in Vitamin D and so I swam toward the rippling sun rays.

When I resurfaced, the exhaustion I'd felt in the aftermath of rescuing Tony had been reduced to a pleasant sleepiness. I changed into my human form and pulled my legs out of the water. The thought of putting my filthy uniform back on wasn't exactly appealing. At least I could go home and take a nap.

"Look who's taking advantage of the Spiral's perks," a sardonic voice said behind me. "The Soul Devourer herself."

I looked up to see the pinched face of Astrid, the local leader of the valkyrie Mean Girls. Her spiderweb-pale hair was braided into rows so tight they gave her eyebrows a lift. When I wasn't feeling harassed by her, I had to admit that she was stunning. Tall and muscular, with the kind of a hawkish face that would look good painted on a vase. She wore an arming doublet and I could smell jasmine wafting off her. A scabbard hung off her hip. Her morning rescue must've been in the Faery Summer Lands. How nice. Tova and Yrsa hovered behind her wide shoulders. Her cronies wore shit-eating grins. Astrid wasn't smiling. She was looking at me with the genuine dislike of someone who thought themselves morally superior. This was probably because, unlike Rudy, she actually *had* seen me eat human souls. She and I were partners at some point. Until she had seen me lose control.

"I thought they'd leave you in Hell this time," Astrid continued. She crossed her arms over her chest. "Where you belong."

Calmly, I pulled myself out of the water and went hunting for my jeans. I squeezed my wet legs into them, then hopped up to zip.

"Hi Astrid," I said. "You look well."

She seethed. Honestly, I might've not been the Spiral's shining jewel, but what was this lady's problem with me?

"And you look like something I found in my chamber pot," she said.

Rubbing the bridge of my nose, I realized I was too tired and beat up for this. I looked Astrid square in the face.

"Did you wait for me to turn back into a human to say that, or?..."

Astrid colored, and I knew I was right on the money. Her anger had the aftertaste of fear. I smiled. Just because she was right about me being a monster didn't mean that she wasn't a massive douche.

"Someday you won't have your betters protecting you," she said. "One more mistake like in Hades, and even the Chief will have to melt your badge."

Two years ago, I'd released my dragon on a rescue mission in Hades. She ate five souls before the ERS operatives wrestled me down. Chief Baran, my boss, had spoken in my defense then, and I kept my job. That's when my mom made the bracelet to keep the dragon contained. Neither one of them could do anything for my nightmares, of course. Or the guilt that made me wake up sweating in the middle of the night. Good thing that, between rescuing souls and my energy drink addiction, I didn't get much sleep.

"Until that happy day," I pointed past her shoulder, "will you be a pal and hand me my bra?"

Her color deepened, and she looked like she'd rather eat a live snake. I walked past her to grab it and snatched my ERS uniform T-shirt next to it. I stuffed my bra and panties into my pockets. Going commando was better than putting those back on after a trip through Hell.

"One day you'll mess up. And I'll be here waiting," Astrid said. Her eyes blazed. "Be sure of it."

I rubbed at the bloodstain on my shirt. "Is this all, or...?"

Behind Astrid's shoulder, Yrsa's freckled nose wrinkled.

"Ophis Lamprou was asking for you," she said. "That's why we—" Astrid glared at her. "What? He was..."

I raised my eyebrows. "Ah. So you're on a peace mission today," I said to Astrid. "Maybe you should switch careers. Better for your blood pressure."

The valkyrie bared her teeth. In one swooping motion, she pulled out her sword. It drew a path in the sunlight.

"Your father is Nidhogg, a vile creature gnawing at the roots of the World Tree," she said. "I'd *love* to gut his spawn."

Well, that escalated fast. On top of wearing nothing but a blood-stained T-shirt and jeans, I'd just left my gun in my holster in the van. Forget the dragon. Right now, I was just a chick with fast healing abilities. And even I couldn't heal a sword sticking out of my chest.

The other two valkyries exchanged a panicked glance. Not that they would report Astrid if she gutted me. I raised my hands in a placating gesture.

"First of all, that's the wrong pantheon. My father and Nidhogg are different—"

The sound of beating wings descended on us. The four of us looked up to see a giant eagle swoop down. It was at least ten feet long, with the wingspan of a dragon. A proper one. It fell onto the ground with a burst of lightning and turned into a guy that looked like he'd stepped out of a body spray commercial. "Diesel: The Power to Pump." Or something. He was heavily tattooed, heavily muscled, and he hulked over all four of us. Grey clouds stirred in his eyes as he glared at me. Instantly, I wished Astrid *had* gutted me.

Zandro Hrom, the arrogant son of Perun—and my ex-boyfriend—was the last person I wanted to see with my panties stuffed into my pocket.

"What is it I hear about you fighting devourers?" he demanded without preamble. "Rudy told me about your scuffle this morning."

Mentally, I cussed out Rudy for his loose tongue. The reaper didn't seem to grasp the conflict of interest between rescuers and demon slayers. You fill one demon full of salt and suddenly you're overstepping into the slayer territory. As if we could do our jobs without running into demons. If it was up to Zandro, the ERS staff would be replaced with overpowered meatheads that couldn't tell a soul from a fart.

"Oh, hello Zan," I said. "I'm good, how are you?"

He ignored me. "I've told you a million times, you run into dangerous demons down there, you call for backup."

"You," I pointed at his chest, "don't have proper clearance. Your entering Hell would be an act of war. You don't want to go to war with Hell over little ole me, do you?"

Sheepishly, Astrid lowered her sword and sheathed it. Her back straightened as she pierced Zan with a look of puppy-dog adoration. Rumors that Zan and I used to date permeated the agency. Maybe there was more to Astrid's hatred of me than just my dragon.

"Slayer Hrom," she said reverently. Yrsa and Tova crossed their fists and bowed to him. I rolled my eyes. I never got the valkyries' hero worship when it came to Zan. He was an excellent demon slayer, sure, but it was more than that. Maybe it was because Perun was the Slavic counterpart of Thor, the Nordic thunder god. Apparently, all the valkyries forgot they weren't interested in men when *he* walked into a room.

Zan nodded at her. "Astrid. Good job on the Fae rescue this morning."

She beamed and bowed over crossed fists.

"Mr. Lamprou was looking for you," she said to me. She suddenly sounded civil. Ha-ha. "He's in the parking lot." Her eyes flicked to Zan and her mouth tightened. "Better not make him wait."

She marched away, taking her entourage with her. The look she gave me on the way out could singe off eyebrows.

I put my palms together and pressed them under my chin. "'Oh, Slayer Hrom, hold me in your powerful arms.'" I sing-sang.

He came to stand over me. His frame blocked out the sun.

"Do you want to die, Green?" he asked.

I inclined my head. "Is that a rhetorical question or a threat?"

"You should've left him there," he said. "Not every soul is a viable rescue."

"Yeah, and who was going to tell his mother we couldn't be bothered to bring her son back?" I asked. "You?"

"You don't have the muscle to deal with devourers," he said. "They would've torn you limb from limb. You want to be soul-dead, Green?"

I shuddered. Being soul-dead meant never going to the Underworld your heart called home. Never being reborn. Instead of being scared, I decided to be mad. I was much better at that. It helped me forget about everything except repaying the massive karmic debt I owed to the universe.

"Maybe if you did your job right and contained the Gates," I said, "I wouldn't have to bust into Hell every five hours."

His lips pressed together. "I am containing them. And you look like you're about to fall apart. Take a vacation, Green."

My cheeks burned. The dark circles under my eyes were a fashion statement, damn it. "We followed protocol. It was a clean rescue, and we have our guy. Now," I said. "Is this everything, or...?"

A silence stretched taut between us. I held his stormy eyes with my own cold look.

"Just don't embarrass Chief Baran," he finally ground out. "He stuck out his neck for you once already."

I silently added "you ungrateful cow" to his lecture.

"Thanks for the reminder," I said. "I'll try to not be an embarrassment."

His jaw clenched. The light caught the back of his head and highlighted the strands of his shoulder-length hair and the scruff on his cheeks. For a second, I forgot how annoyed I was. He was hot. *Damn* hot. It was no wonder the women of the agency stumbled out of their heels when he walked by. A long time ago, when we were seventeen, I'd spent hours exploring the strong planes of his face, and the firm line of his upper lip with my mouth. That damned dimple on his squared chin. That was before he found out that our fathers were mortal enemies and dumped me. It was bad enough to be reminded of my monstrosity by the valkyries. Zan was walking proof that I was unworthy in the eyes of all the

Spiral's supernaturals. I could feel the itch of my horns at the top of my head. As if sensing them, too, his eyes flicked to my hair. My teeth ground together.

I made myself straighten my back. I was a professional, damn it. "I will write a report for Chief Baran," I said evenly. "Now, if you're done berating me," I pushed past him toward the door, "I have an appointment with someone who's not a jerk."

He looked ready to say something else. Instead, he watched me leave, expression unreadable.

3

I WALKED PAST THE ERS station and toward the car park. The vans were parked at their stations. They'd been scrubbed clean by the department brownies. The house sprites did a good job, I thought, as I walked to the spot that contained my and Rudy's van. The soot was rubbed clean off and the rims sparkled. Every van was precious. Wired and warded for travel between the human world and the Underworlds, they followed invisible pipelines that connected the universe. It was a design that made Reno's ERS the Spiral's pride and joy. A creak of tiny wheels told me I wasn't alone. I turned around in time to see a man roll out from under one of the vans on a shop creeper.

He wore a pair of greasy overalls without a shirt underneath. His hairy chest would make a werewolf jealous. Ancient sunglasses sat on the tip of his prominent nose. His mustache was long enough to drape around his chin.

My face split into my first genuine smile today. The sour mood that Zan had left me in was rapidly evaporating.

"Uncle Ophis!" I said as he scampered up with a dexterity that didn't match his middle-aged appearance. "I thought you were in Utah until the summer."

He kicked the creeper back under the van, and yanked his glasses off his face. Pulling out a filthy hanky, he began polishing the lenses. I wasn't sure it was making them any cleaner.

"You children and your hard riding," he shook an oil-stained finger in front of my face, "if I didn't come to maintain these vans, you'd ride the pipelines to the bone."

I grinned at my old friend. When I'd joined the force years ago, he was the one who made me feel like I'd belonged. He was also the descendant of Ananke the snake. Rumors had it he could turn into a serpent himself. I wondered if that's why he'd taken a liking to me.

Ophis Lamprou was the reason Reno's ERS team had the advantage over the East coast branch. He was the genius behind the vans being able to travel down into Hell. The ghost in the machine. The secret sauce.

"You know us Whipper-Snappers," I said brightly. "We've got fire under the hood."

He chortled. "*You* surely do, Daughter of Veles. If I needed a getaway car stealing golden apples from Hera, I'd call you."

My shrug was deliberately casual. "That's why they keep me around."

He gave me a knowing smile. "That and more."

I cleared my throat. "You were looking for me?"

"Yes," he shoved his glasses back up his nose, "I have a message for you." Digging through the pockets of his overalls, he pulled out something small and wrapped in plastic. "Here."

I let the object fall into my hand. "A fortune cookie?"

"I was having dinner with a friend." He sniffed. "In one of those gyro places you Americans call "Greek."

I grinned. "You were on a date?"

Mustache swaying, he jerked his chin impatiently. "She is a seer. When we got the check, they gave her this cookie. She handed it to me, said it wasn't meant for her, but for you."

Frowning, I tugged off the plastic and broke the cookie open.

"An exciting opportunity lies ahead of you." I read out loud. Cocking an eyebrow, I looked up at the man. "That's nice."

The older plumber shrugged his skinny shoulders. "Unripe grape gets as sweet as honey at a slow pace. You'll figure it out."

Whatever that meant.

The Spiral's elevator took me back up to the Space Whale. From there, I walked across the bridge that stretched over the Truckee River. The water splashed over shallows and turned a black-green over depths. The heat was just beginning to bake my shoulders when I made it to my apartment complex. I live in one of the

Towers that overlooks the Wingfield Park. No, *not* the nice one. Another elevator ride later, I was jamming my keys into my lock.

My one-bedroom apartment greeted me with the smell of greasy takeout. I kicked off my Docs and cringed at the mess in front of me. I had lived by myself for five years, and I was yet to figure out a way to make my apartment resemble a home. Resigned, I took to cleaning the kitchen. Yesterday's Pad Thai had solidified into a mass of inedible pasta and spicy peanut sauce. I put the food in the garbage and dug through my fridge. The empty shelves left much to be desired, but the freezer lifted my spirits. I dug out a bean burrito from the recess of the shelf and microwaved it. The real score was the hot sauce packets left over from last week's takeout. I squirted them over the tortilla.

I'm not much of a housekeeper. Or a house person, really. Maybe *I* should get a brownie. If you asked my mother, she'd say I needed a boyfriend. I would agree if it wasn't for the fact that I couldn't keep one to save my life. Maybe it was the crazy work hours, maybe it was my shitty attitude, but the door to my apartment had become a high-security vault. I'd dated here and there, sure. A girl has her needs. But as far as someone who I could curl up and watch a movie with, my couch stayed cold. It was a gripe I'd made peace with long ago. My life was Hell, death, and angry valkyries. And that was totally fine. Totally.

A soft meowing called to me as I plopped down on the couch.

"Hey, Mittens," I said.

I shimmering shape appeared out of the wall. Mittens—my tabby who got his name for his white "socks"—had died when I was ten. I had cried for days before I found out that being related to the god of an Underworld has its perks. When my furry little bestie didn't want to go over the Rainbow Bridge, he simply stayed. Unlike souls still attached to bodies, ghosts don't dissolve into the universe. Spirits are funny like that. I patted my lap and his weightless form hopped up. His ectoplasmic body had a luminescent shimmer which resembled my dragon. I could barely feel his fur as I ran my fingers through it. It was as fine as dandelion fluff. Who needed a boyfriend when I had my fur baby? Petting him, I finished my burrito and gave him a little kiss on the forehead. If you don't take time to kiss your ghost kitty every day, what are you even doing with your life?

The murderous April sun finally relented and gave way to a crimson sunset. I took the fortune out of my pocket and smoothed it out on the coffee table. Uncle Ophis was a strange ancient dude, but he wasn't someone to take lightly. I read the message over and over until my eyes got too sticky to keep open. It was still nonsense. Finally, not even the caffeine wave I was riding could cut through fatigue. I barely had enough sense to set down my plate before exhaustion pulled me into the cushions.

I woke up to someone knocking on the door. Mittens meowed, scandalized, and bounced off my lap. I blinked, disoriented, at the pale sky outside the window. It was sunset when I'd fallen asleep. Had I been out for less than an hour, or...? My answer waited for me on my cell phone. It was six in the morning, and I had twenty-three missed calls. Adrenaline slapped me awake, and I scrambled to my feet. The knocking at my door turned into hammering. This had to be bad news. No one visited me.

"Coming, coming!" I called as I stumbled to the door.

Rudy stood in the hallway, his arms crossed over his chest. He wore a blue Nike hoodie that was supposed to make him look more human, I guess. Instead, it highlighted just how inhuman—and honestly a bit creepy—his beauty was. Like a death's head moth trapped in a mason jar. He wore his leather biking gloves and carried a black helmet under his arm. It had a crossbones design on it. How original.

"Did those devourers eat your fingers?" he asked.

Eyelids sticky, I blinked. "What?"

"Because you can't be bothered to answer your phone."

"I'm sorry—"

He moved to shoulder past me when his foot snagged something by my door. I stooped and picked up a brown bag. The top was rolled up and it had an oil stain on the side. Shaking my head, I smiled. Inside were some carefully sliced bits of chicken and some mashed potatoes. Perfect for a spoiled cat.

"It's my neighbor, Mrs. Lehmann," I said. "She can see ghosts, but she's a bit out of it. She thinks Mittens is alive, and I don't want to disappoint her—"

I caught Rudy's dark look and shut my mouth. Instantly, it occurred to me that the reaper only made house calls to one sort of people. The *dead*.

"What's going on?"

He stepped into my living room. The wards over the entry way buzzed. I had made Rudy one of the people who could pass through, just in case. Not that I ever expected him to actually *come*. Usually, unexpected visitors found themselves paralyzed from the waist down. That's how I liked them. I let out a belated sound of protest.

"I don't think I've ever been to your place before," he said. "I think I know why." His eyes went to my fallen-in couch. "You should toss that out. I can see the springs."

Crossing my arms, I glared at him. "How about I toss *you* out?" I said. "Why are you here? What happened?"

"The devourers, that's what," he said.

I frowned. "The ones from yesterday?"

"Hard to tell. There's been a breakout. Somehow, a lot of them got through the Gates after us."

My fingers on the bag, I stiffened.

"Was it Tony's summoning?" I asked.

He shrugged. "Tony opened a doorway, and we threw a torch into their nest. They were clearly angry. Either way, it doesn't matter. Chief Baran wants us in his office. Now."

Dread dragged through my core. Devourers were Beelzebub's demons, and he was a Prince of Hell and the demon of gluttony. A personification of all-consuming hunger. Which meant that no one in the Reno area was safe—no man, woman, or child.

"How many demons, Rudy?"

For the first time, Rudy didn't answer immediately. He tapped his foot and his skull flashed white under his skin.

His shoulders rose and stiffened. It was a slight movement, but I knew his tells. The reaper was anxious. Which meant that I needed to be screaming and running down the hall.

"At least fifty," he said.

4

W E RODE RUDY'S SLEEK Ducati Diavel back to the Spiral headquarters. I know little about motorcycles, but his was an onyx-black beauty that was polished to a ridiculous shine. You'd think someone who reaped souls would go with a Harley and not a modern marvel. I had taken exactly ten minutes to shower, shrug into a fresh pair of tank top and jeans, and slide the salt gun into my holster. I added other cartridges onto my belt, too. Iron pellets and silver shavings. We weren't going against the Fae or werewolves, but no amount of caution was too much for devourers. I slammed down a Red Bull to clear the cobwebs. My forehead itched as my horns responded to my nerves. Half the missed calls on my phone were from Chief Baran. I didn't even bother calling him back. He could yell at me at me much more effectively in person.

This time, we didn't go down to the ERS tunnels. Neither did we need to contend with traffic or silly laws like physics. Rudy drove right over the water of the river and through the metal of the bridges that covered the short distance between my place and the City Hall. No wonder Astrid was turning in her sleep as she imagined me partnered with Rudy. Reaper magic was terrifyingly cool. Both figuratively and literally. I almost froze to his back on the way there.

The Spiral office is in another layer of reality. We might've entered Reno's City Hall, but we ended up in the Reno division of the Spiral.

We marched into the front lobby.

The golden ammonite, the symbol of the Spiral, glistened over a glass-and-steel reception desk. Modern couches stretched under a giant hologram of the World Tree that rose up to the glass ceiling. The real Tree was much bigger, of course. In fact, it was immeasurably huge. Its branches connected the human world and the supernatural ones. No matter what plane it appeared on, it led to different pantheons. The Nords called it Yggdrasil, the Slavs called it the Great Oak, and Hindus called it Ashvatta. It didn't change its location or its purpose as the unifying force between the worlds. The part I was most familiar with was the roots. While the branches stretched toward the pantheons, the roots led to the Underworlds. Reno was located over the roots that led to a variety of Underworlds. The lineup included Hell, Duat, Hades, and a variety of the nastier Fae planes. Nav—my father's Underworld—was on the list. Enter the ERS department and yours truly as a soul rescuer, stage right.

The undine secretary stared at me with eyes devoid of pupils. She scanned me from my blood-stained boots to my ERS-issue tank top that had seen too many wash cycles. At least I'd had the sense to run a brush through my tangle of black hair. Her delicate gills flared over her designer earrings and her green, webbed fingers tapped the numbers on the receiver.

"Hey, Seline," I said. Her response was a slow blink.

Rudy walked over to the desk, his own boots sparkling-clean and clicking on the tiles.

"Rescuers Green and Mort here to see Chief Baran."

She gave him another long stare. I wondered if she smiled at anyone but the executives. Finally, she picked up the phone.

"They're here," she said into the receiver.

We were expected. Of course.

The elevator took us up to the top floor where the big wigs—primarily my boss—had nested between the rows of cubicles. Backs straight and heads held high, we walked past the whispering paper-pushers. I didn't have the best reputation, but walking in with Rudy gave me an invisible layer of protection only reaper royalty could provide. I was grateful, of course. I didn't have any illusions that he wasn't one reason I was employed. Well, him and Chief Baran. Who presently was seething with rage and regretting ever sticking up for me after Hades. Probably. I made myself go ahead of Rudy and knock on the door. If we were somehow to blame for the demons breaking through, it should be my ass on the line. I made sure that my van's key fob was in the pocket of my jeans. Whatever Chief had to say, we'd make it right. As soon as the conference was over, we'd summon the van onto the street and be off. No time to waste with so many demons to track down.

"Come in," my boss's thick voice called through the door.

Swallowing, I steeled myself. I pushed the door open.

Chief Baran was leaning against his desk. He was a handsome middle-aged man with a neatly trimmed beard that stretched a little too high into his hair. A pair of budding horns gave away his satyr blood. Unlike me, he wore his horns proudly. His clever, lean body seemed to escape the ravages of a desk job. Even with his best years behind him, our handsome boss was kind of "daddy." The office girls weren't shy about flirting with him. Rumor had it, he was a high-ranking rescuer in New York in his younger days. When the Reno branch received clearance to rescue from Hell several years ago, he volunteered to transfer and run the department. Lucky, too. It was only two weeks before my dragon had decided to get snacky in Hades.

My mouth moved to smile when I saw he wasn't the only man in the room.

The head of the Spiral's ERS sector, Director Stonefield, glowered at me from the Chief's chair. His muscled arms spilled out of his rolled-up sleeves. Unlike Baran, his younger years seemed decades past him as his gut propped up the Chief's desk and his scalp reflected the fluorescent light. He was part djinn and wasn't shy about throwing fire around. His narrow eyes nailed me to the floor.

"Green," he growled. "You have some nerve not answering the calls of your superiors at a time like this."

I swallowed and suppressed an urge to click my heels like I was in the army.

"Director," I said. "I was—"

"Resting," Rudy said behind me. With a sure hand, he closed the door in the faces of multiple curious office workers who had craned their necks to get a glimpse of the drama. "We were ambushed by devourers on our rescue yesterday. I'm afraid the extraction had cost us."

I threw Rudy a grateful look. His chilly demeanor was habitually unimpressed by anyone's high rank.

Stonefield ground his teeth. "Well, I'm glad you're well-rested, Green. It seems that your antics have angered a nest."

Turning toward a golden cube with an ammonite carved on it, he pushed a panel. The device spat out a grainy hologram that flickered in front our faces.

I immediately recognized devourers. Hunched over, they wore something that resembled human clothes. If the clothes were stolen from an eighteenth-century grave. The shreds of fabric did little to hide the bulge of the bellies and the claws that were so long they almost dragged on the ground. Their eyes were almost human. This, above all else, made them incredibly terrifying. It was human greed, of course. The humans who, thousands of years ago, had believed enough in Beelzebub to manifest him. The image moved, and we watched as devourers spilled out of the hole in the ground. They had nets slung over their backs. Squinting, I tried to make out what they were carrying, but it was too far away.

The location was clear enough. I had only used it to land us in Reno yesterday, after all.

"This is three hours ago," Chief Baran said. His voice was silky-smooth, and he didn't sound angry, just matter-of-fact. "Twelve hours after you entered the human world with Tony Alvarez." He clicked a remote control, and the image changed to another that looked even lower quality. In this one, the devourers were entering a line of trees. I couldn't see properly how many there were. "This is one hour ago." He ran his hand through his beard.

"Explain yourself, Green," Stonefield said. "Did one of them follow you? Did you check under the van before you'd made it out with the soul?" he asked. "Could one of them enter the human world and draw a seal to summon the others?"

Rudy and I exchanged glances. We shook our heads in unison.

I answered for both of us. "We followed the safety protocol, Sir. Every possible hiding place was checked before the exit from the Gates."

He moved his jowls, but I could see that he believed us. Good. Rudy and I were many things, but we weren't sloppy.

"With all due respect," I continued. "That looks like a physical hole. Seals don't blow up like that, they pull demons through by metaphysical pathways channeled by the human's belief. This looks like—"

"I think I know better than you what this looks like," Stonefield growled. "Zandro Hrom informed me that you engaged in a physical altercation with devourers. Now, at least fifty of them are roaming Nevada."

I swore under my breath. Hrom. *Of course.* "I don't know—"

"What *I* know is they broke out at the site of your exit." He cut off the hologram. "We will work with the demon slayers to find and apprehend the devourers."

"We can help," I said quickly. This was my one chance to get ahead of Hrom and his army of thugs. "Rudy and I can find them using the methods we employ in Hell. We can get to them before—"

Stonefield purpled, and the words died on my tongue. Chief Baran answered for him.

"You two have been suspended until the matter is resolved." He limped around the desk and picked up a folder. His old rescue injury must've been giving him grief. Seeing my stricken expression, he softened his voice. "Take a day, Green. You two have been working yourself to the ground."

"Chief—"

Director Stonefield rose from the Chief's chair and to his full height. Instantly, the surrounding air warmed. Embers flickered in his eyes.

"You are dismissed," he ground out. I saw flame between his teeth. "If I find you anywhere near the Spiral before the devourers are caught, you'll be out of a job."

Cheeks flushing, I looked up at the man. He's been looking for an excuse to fire me for two years. Now, he was just waiting for me to hand him one on a silver platter. My horns itched to come out. If I hadn't let my dragon swim yesterday, I probably wouldn't have been able to contain her.

"Yes, Sir," I finally ground out. Red framing my vision, I followed Rudy into the hallway.

Being a rescuer wasn't just my job. It's what I'd wanted to do from the marrow of my bones. From the time I saw my best friend get destroyed by a demon and had no one to blame but myself. Rudy and I were the best trackers in the ERS. I knew we could find the demons before Hrom did.

"Green!" the Chief's voice called from behind me.

I turned around to see him coming after me. The folder I had abandoned was clutched in his hand. His limp was more pronounced now that he was agitated. I made myself take a deep breath. Chief Baran had earned my respect many times over. Rudy raised his eyebrows at me and I gave him a quick nod to go on without me.

"Thank you, Chief," I reached out my hand for the paperwork. "I didn't mean to leave this."

He jerked his head toward the window, and away from the prying eyes of the office staff. Frowning, I followed him.

His hand rested on my shoulder, and he leaned closer. I could smell the sharpness of his aftershave and the subtle, but not unpleasant, scent of his sweat. His deep brown eyes burrowed into mine.

"This is nothing personal," he said. "I hope you know that."

I swallowed a sudden burst of heat behind my eyes. My eyes dropped to his vested chest. "You're my best rescuer, Green," he said. "Don't doubt it. What happened yesterday isn't your fault."

"I know," I said through the lump in my throat. "But Stonefield seems to not agree."

"Being a rescuer takes a toll. Emotionally and physically. Sometimes it's the job, and sometimes it's the politics," he said. "Two years ago, I kept you in this job for a reason. Your passion is rare, and I've only seen one person with such spirit before."

I snorted. "Astrid?"

Baran smiled. "Myself." He pushed the folder at me and I took it. "I'll keep you posted, okay?" He winked. "Don't tell Stonefield. Let's keep both of us from getting fired."

I nodded. "Thank you, Chief."

Outside, Rudy waited for me by the bike. I didn't ask him how he got there so fast. Reapers have their way. Presumably ready to take me home, he moved to mount it.

"Hang on!" I said.

Choosing my next words carefully, I looked at Rudy. "Something isn't right," I said. "You know we didn't mess up."

He shrugged. "Of course we didn't."

Tapping my boot on the asphalt, I thought about what Chief Baran said. Two years ago, he gave me a second chance at being a rescuer. I didn't want to jeopardize that. But fifty devourers were a small army. If they weren't stopped, they could wipe out a suburban neighborhood. How had they gotten out if they hadn't followed us?

"Can we go to the site?" I asked. "Where the devourers broke through?"

He gave me an incredulous look. "The Chief told us to stay put."

"I know," I said. "I just want to take a quick look." I shivered, suddenly chilly. "What if we did mess up, Rudy?" When he didn't answer, I pressed. "I just want to see if it was a stowaway demon summoner or something else."

I waited, knowing I'd pressed the right buttons. According to his pride, the reaper didn't *make* mistakes.

After a long pause, he handed me my helmet. "If this gets you off my back."

5

We arrived at the breakout site to find the busy bees of human emergency services taping off the area. Fire trucks, police cars, and public works crowded the hole in the ground. I squinted past the yellow flags fluttering in the wind. The asphalt had collapsed into a sinkhole in the middle of the road. Groups of curious passersby crowded the area as they rubbernecked over the closures. We weren't close enough to see it properly.

I wasn't playing at getting myself fired. Last thing I wanted was to get Chief Baran in trouble. All I wanted to do was see what was going on at the breakout site.

"Right," I said. "In and out."

Rudy gave me a rare, wicked smile. "See you on the other side."

He blurred in my vision as his blue hoodie shifted into a robe. I've seen the transformation before, but it still creeped me out. The worst was his face as it lost its flesh. His skull grinned back at me. Luckily, I didn't look at it for too long. With a ripple that I could feel crawl over my skin, the universe swallowed him whole. The Death's mantle rendered him completely invisible. It also left me behind to fend for myself.

"Hey! No fair."

I eyed the burly backs of the firefighters. They were idling by the truck, looking utterly bored in their state-issued uniforms. Their well-muscled physique definitely drew my eye to the places *other* than the demon break out site. Somehow, I needed to make it past the wall of hotness without getting distracted. Or getting caught.

I pulled my ERS badge out of my pocket. It was similar enough to the EMT badge even I could manage a minor illusion to alter it. The Orphic egg disappeared and was replaced by a snake curled around a staff. The gold of the Spiral could easily be mistaken for brass. Straightening my spine, I sauntered over to lazing firefighters like I belonged there.

"Gentlemen," I lifted the yellow tape and stepped through. "Working hard or hardly working?"

At their questioning glance I raised my "EMT" badge. Then, to really grease it up, I gave the tallest piece of man-candy a wink. He grinned with a row of white teeth, his eyes drifting down my body. The others followed suit, and I felt myself warm at the attention.

"Just checking for accidental falls," I told them.

They looked dubious at that.

"There isn't anyone down there," the head guy said.

"Really?" My eyes drifted over to the sinkhole. I could see the ripple, like a flaw in blown glass, where Rudy was doing his inspection. "Mind if I check? Sometimes these things can swallow a car whole in under twenty-five seconds." I gave them my most charming smile. "The department likes to be thorough. You know how bosses are. Paranoia pays the bills."

They exchanged glances. I tried to look as bored and as boring as possible. Just another city grunt, doing her job. Finally, they shrugged and gave me space to step between them.

Relieved, I walked past.

"I owe you a coffee!" I called over my shoulder.

"How about I buy you one?" my tall piece of man-candy called after me. I grinned over my shoulder and gave him a queenly wave.

The sinkhole was twenty feet long and about fifteen feet wide. Inside, the water of the Truckee River had already claimed the depth, making it impossible to see to the bottom. My demi blood could perceive what the mortal eyes couldn't—the water was thick and shimmering-black, like nail polish. I had never seen a breakout site before. It seemed to swallow light.

I frowned. "Do you smell burning?" I asked Rudy.

"It's coming from Hell," his incorporeal voice replied. "Of course it smells like burning."

I shook my head. "No, it's artificial." It was a familiar smell, like burning engine oil. I'd smelled enough of it in my childhood as our van rolled for miles and miles with a mom who wasn't exactly a whiz under the hood. My eyes drifted to the edges of the sinkhole. They were singed. Running my fingers over the black, I sniffed. A sharp smell that resembled smoldering rubber hit my nostrils.

I frowned. "This didn't come from Hell," I said to Rudy. "I'm no explosives expert, but this smells like something from the human world."

Out of the corner of my eye, I saw a flash of Rudy's skull. He knelt next to me to see for himself.

"Well, Green," he said after a pause. "That can only mean one thing."

I nodded. "The demons didn't break out on their own. Maybe they did follow us up but we couldn't have taken them all the way through." I wiped my hand on my jeans. "They had help."

A flicker of movement caught my eye. It came from under the lip of the broken asphalt. I whirled toward it, hand going to my holster.

"Did you see—?"

Black blurred in my vision. A glimpse of flesh-tearing claws. The firefighters were wrong. There was someone in the sinkhole. Except it wasn't an unfortunate Reno citizen.

Pain slashed down my ribs before I could pull out my gun. Then, it was in my hand and I was firing at the barreling shadow. I heard a howl, but a slowing of the creature did not accompany it. The form leapt out from under the ledge even faster.

The devourer was seven feet tall. Lanky and hunched over, its claws dragged on the ground. Its face was a multitude of scars. There were so many of them that it looked like a burn victim. It had lashed a net onto its back. Beneath the enchanted binds, I could see a shimmering blob.

A human soul. I swallowed.

Souls that had been dead for a long time lost their once-human shape. They resembled sticky wisps of light that looked a bit fleshy in the human world. This was why the devourers broke out. Something told me they weren't going to sell them at the Demon Bazaar.

Beelzebub's demon raised his claws up off the ground and looked at me with hungry, blood-filled eyes.

I unloaded another round of salt into him. He doubled over and hissed.

"Get back!" Rudy yelled. The Death's mantle slid off him as he came into view, his ulaks bared along with his human teeth. I hesitated as he jumped in front of me. Rudy could take down a devourer. He'd done as much when we crashed the nest yesterday. But my eyes lingered on the soul in the net. I needed to get to it before Rudy accidentally slashed the bounds and the soul dissipated into the universe.

"Hang on!" I fell to the left and began sidestepping into its blind spot. "Distract him!"

"What the Hell, Green?!"

He did as he was told, though, his ulaks flashing in the sun. The demon's jaw unhinged and pin-points of shark-like teeth bared at the reaper. I didn't have time to be terrified. While its back was turned, I leapt forward and elbowed it in the jaw. I could feel the blood pooling into my jeans as the movement tore my ribcage wound wider. What I was doing was excruciatingly stupid.

Chief Baran was right. I was already worn to the bone with driving the van on a near-daily basis. But all I saw was the soul. All my dragon saw was the soul. Its writhing luminescent mass didn't belong here. It was my duty to right the wrong. I grabbed at the thong that tied the soul to the demon's shoulder and yanked. The soul came free as I fell from him. Inside my skin, the dragon roared. My horns burst out of my skull with dizzying relief. Rudy's ulaks criss-crossed and slashed the devourer across the chest. With a swipe of its claws, it made the reaper fly. Finally, I got the full brunt of the devourer's attention.

Clutching the soul to my chest like it was a glowing treasure, I backed away. My gun stretched out before me as I aimed it at the demon's face.

"It's not yours," I said. "Come for it at your peril." The growl coming out of my throat was not my human voice, but my dragon's. It felt good, so good, to let her spill out of my pores. My hand holding the gun was covered in tiny translucent scales. If only I let her out, I could crush the demon. It took all of my mental clarity to wrestle her down. Behind the devourer, Rudy leapt up from the ground. His form dissolved into the air as he put on his Death's mantle. Three seconds was all I needed. Three seconds until-

"What the fuck!" a voice called behind me.

My heart sank as the devourer's piglet eyes snapped in its direction. The firefighters chose the wrong moment to take a break from their break. The demon's breathing slowed. No one's more delicious to devourers than a fresh human. Not even a soul, especially when it's being inconveniently guarded by a dragon shifter.

As if smelling the firefighter's fear, a second shape slipped out of the sinkhole. Two devourers. I swore under my breath. So much for Rudy's ambush. My gun wavered between them, but they weren't looking at me.

Looking back, I wasn't surprised to see the firefighter standing closest was the cute one. The one who'd teased me about a coffee date. There was a gun in his hand. Unlike mine, he'd loaded it with regular bullets. Why did he have it? He was much better off with a fire axe.

"Don't!" I yelped at him.

It was too late. His eyes bulging with the shock of a human who saw something he never believed existed, he emptied a round in the devourer's belly. He roared, and I shot at the other one blindly, wanting to give the guy a moment's distraction. The bullets didn't impede the devourer like the salt did. What they did was invigorate him.

It barely looked at me as it swiped my gun out of my hand. It clattered to the ground. The soul was torn from my arms.

"No!"

With a sickening slurp, the devourer's shark teeth sank into the soul. Its body swelled in size and it roared. The power of a single human life made its muscles ripple and its limbs double in size. There was an answering howl somewhere from a distance. Was a giant wolf about to join the party? My eyes fell to the soul at my feet. It flapped in the wind like a plastic shopping bag.

Dry and empty. A soul husk, it was called. I had only seen one once before, when I was twelve, and my life had split into a "before" and an "after". My stomach turning, I scrambled for my gun.

The super-sized devourer leapt at the firefighter. I pulled myself onto one knee and shot at his back. Salt slowed it down, but now it was even more horrible.

Instead of one quick slash, the devourer's claw slowed as it gutted the guy from groin to chest. Its back blocked me from seeing his guts splashing onto the asphalt. I heard it, though, the sickening squelch of organs, the sound of his heavy body hitting the road. The devourer paused over the still-twitching man and drew in a deep, indulgent breath. Then, it stepped toward the other fighters. There was yelling and scrambling. My gun clicked. I was out of salt rounds.

There was a growl behind me and I glanced back to see the second devourer scream and lash out at Rudy. It overshot and missed. Demon blood was purplish-red like an old bruise. It splashed at the reaper's feet.

There were other sounds, like balloons popping. They were coming from all around us. Commands filled the air.

Demon slayers. They'd finally shown up to contain the scene.

My eyes searched for Zan when an invisible hand pulled me away from the firefighter's body.

"We're suspended, remember?" Rudy hissed into my ear. "Move it, or lose your badge!"

The firefighters realized that shooting an abomination was useless. They ran for their lives. There were yells coming from all around us. Demon slayer arrows dotted the ground.

"They have souls," I sniveled as Rudy pulled me past the chaos and toward his bike. "They have souls, Rudy!"

"I know," my partner's voice was soft. "Now, go!"

Slipping on my own blood, I went.

6

Henry sniffed as he smeared salve over the slash on my ribs. It smelled like peppermint and sea weed. Instantly, the agony of the shredded tissue was replaced was a dull, pulsing pain. I sagged against the chair.

The selkie smiled at me with a row of narrow teeth.

"Lucky you've got demi blood," he said as he taped gauze over the wound. "This would put me on my ass for a week. You? Back to kicking ass tomorrow."

I nodded, grateful, and pulled down my tank top. It was dark with dried blood.

"We were never here, alright?" I said. My eyes flicked to Rudy who had just walked back into the room, phone in hand. He leaned against the door frame with an unreadable expression.

Henry raised his rubber-gloved hands. "Doctor-patient confidentiality."

We were sitting in the ERS medical quarter. It was abandoned. Everyone had gone to contain the damage and the bodies at the sinkhole. The other Heal Hands had gone to see if they could save anyone. I remembered the firefighter and shuddered.

"Thanks, Henry."

The Heal Hand gave me a salute and walked over to the washing station. I waited for him to turn on the tap.

"We have to tell Chief Baran about the souls," I said to Rudy.

He raised his phone. "I just did."

I gaped at him. "Did you—"

Shrugging, he put the phone in his pocket. "I told him we went against his explicit orders."

"Rudy!"

The corner of his mouth lifted. "Reaper grapevine. I told him that one of my colleagues saw a devourer touting a soul and called it in. They also found that husk at the sinkhole."

I nodded, hope rising in my chest. "And?"

"Stonefield is sure we caused the break out. He won't budge," Rudy said. "He assigned Astrid onto Zandro's team to get the souls."

I rubbed my temples. Of course. Astrid must be happy with me off the case and Zan's ass in near proximity. All the better to kiss it.

"Chief Baran told me to remind you to "save your talents for when they matter." Rudy's forehead creased. "Never took him for a cryptic." He pushed away from the door frame. "I'll get us some food. You like that greasy human stuff, right?"

Nodding, I gave him a weak smile. "Extra spicy."

Wrapping my arms around myself, I stared at the beige, tiled floor. The dead firefighter floated behind my eyelids when I closed my eyes. Bile rose to my throat when I remembered that he wasn't even the one who was worst off.

The soul that the devourer had drained would never be reborn. It was gone from the universe. Whoever that person had been, they were erased. Just remembering it flutter on the asphalt like a dead jellyfish made angry tears crawl up my throat. I remember the last time I saw one, all too well.

When I was twelve, my mom and I spent a year in a holistic commune. Demon summoning wasn't exactly on my agenda then. If anything, I wanted to be a healer like my mom, except that I found her so embarrassing then. The advice that she gave people seemed so goofy: "pray to Hecate during a full moon over this obsidian, and the pain will abate." I thought all that healer stuff was tacky. Until Lizzy got interested in it.

Those who had best friends growing up will understand this: Lizzy was my first love. Everything about her was bold and curvaceous—her large brown eyes and soft plump body that just hinted at approaching womanhood. Unlike me, who was all angles with unnervingly bright blue eyes, she was gentle and everyone always did everything she wanted. Her entire demeanor seemed to exist just to be the opposite of mine. One look at me and people dismissed me as difficult. The other kids in the commune avoided me. You'd think I'd resent her, but my tomboy heart was smitten. She wasn't scared of me, like the others; she thought I was kind of cool. I felt kind of cool when I was around her. I wanted to do everything to protect her. But my first desire had been to impress her. When she suddenly became interested in my mother's spell books, I was more than eager to "borrow" them for her. I loved catching her interest by doing the spells together. This is where I found out that I was a lot more like my mother than I cared to admit. Spells just worked for me. Suddenly, I was the center of Lizzy's fascination. I adored the way she looked at me when I summoned wood sprites or charged crystals to make her skin literally glow for an entire day of wearing them. We found more and more spell books, and light and magic constantly filled the abandoned hut we met in.

One day, she came to me, her heart-shaped face flushed with excitement. She carried a book in her hand. I didn't recognize the title. Plopping on Himalayan pillows next to me, she flipped open the first page. It was a book on Demonology. One of the real ones. My mouth dried as she leafed through. I could tell that it was real because of the magic that dripped from it. As my demi blood stripped away the illusion, I saw it leak with dark red energy like congealed blood.

"Where did you get this?" I asked Lizzy.

She gathered her feet under and beamed with pride. "Found it in the empty cabin. The one that Rainbow Dreads lived in."

Rainbow Dreads was the nickname we gave to the occupant who had made the choice to weave rainbow threads into his matted hair. I remembered his slightly brittle smile and too-thin frame. He always seemed in a hurry, talked too fast. We'd seen his type come and go before. A drifter. He didn't exactly strike me as a practitioner.

"We should leave it alone, Liz," I'd said to her. My mouth tasted bitter just looking at it. "It's not safe."

"But—" she'd looked at me with her large doe eyes. I don't think I had ever told her "No" before. "I had to dig under the floorboards to get it."

I shook my head. "This one is dangerous."

She pouted. "It's just a book."

Oh, but it wasn't. I already knew that. The sensible thing to do was give it to my mom. Or chuck it in the fire. I wasn't sensible. All I saw was Lizzy's pleading eyes and her expectations to see something amazing. I had been upping the stakes by casting spells more and more fantastical. Humans get addicted to magic. I didn't know that then.

It took me all of three days to crack. Her approval was the only thing that I'd craved in my young life.

The day we summoned Asmoday, candles flickered around our pillows. Lizzy lit the incense, and it wrapped us in the scent of smoky cloves. I opened the book at the beginning and started leafing through it with hesitant fingers.

"Maybe we can do a small one?" I said, trying to keep the pleading out of my voice. "Just to start?"

She grabbed the book from my hands. "I already know the perfect one!" she plucked the pages to the middle. "This one."

Setting it down, she stabbed her finger in the middle. I looked at the face of a demon. A furry face and owlish eyes swam up at me from the page. One of his legs was human and the other a hoof. Three animal parts grew out of his shoulders: a bull's head, a ram's head, and a snake's tail.

"He helps you find treasure and grants wishes," Lizzy said in a hushed, excited voice.

I took a deep breath. "This probably isn't even real," I said in a light voice. "Just some nonsense they wrote for guys like Rainbow Dreads."

She scanned over me with a calculating eye. "I thought you were cool, Chrys."

I deflated where I sat. She was the only one who wasn't afraid of me, or avoided me because I was weird. The thought of losing that made my heart sink. "I am."

"Good!" she pushed the book toward me. "Draw the seal then."

She handed me a chalk and pointed to the floor.

"I'd wish for mom to move us to the city," she said. I frowned, and she added quickly: "I'll take you with me! We'll go to Starbucks! All four of us!"

The thought of my mom sitting in Starbucks made me snicker.

"Come on," she nudged.

Book in one hand, I drew.

At first, the lines came shaky and unsure, but my hand began drawing smoothly like I had done it hundreds of times.

"Whoa," Lizzy said. "I knew you'd be amazing."

It took me close to a half an hour to finish the seal. The symbols were unfamiliar, but they sang in my blood.

It was as if I'd known them without knowing them. Lizzy's eyes shone, and I felt a sense of pride. If someone as special as she saw me as someone worthy of attention, maybe I actually was. At the outer ring of the circle, I purposefully fudged a line. I wanted to impress Lizzy, but my core was taut, like a string.

I sat back down on the pillows. Lizzy's face swam in the incense smoke in front of me.

"See?" I said. "Nothing." I tossed the book aside. "It's a dummy."

Something pulsed inside my chest, making me see double. I gasped and clutched my T-shirt.

"What was that?" Lizzy pulled up her feet. "Something just—"

It happened again, and I saw a ghostly shape rise out of my chest. It wasn't fully formed. All I saw was scales and a glimpse of a claw. It was ephemeral, like Casper from that movie. I was too terrified to scream. The claw reached toward the seal. It made it glow. The line that I'd messed up on purpose righted itself.

The rings I drew within each other turned like a safe lock dialing the code. Something cracked as they aligned. Lizzy squealed in terror and awe. I just felt terror. The thing that came out of my chest was gone now. A headache split my forehead. I drew my hand up and felt... Horns. This is when I screamed. A roar that came from the seal soon drowned my scream.

A hairy form burst out in the middle of it and I saw it rise over our bodies. The demon was easily seven feet tall and had three heads. Two animal heads burst out on either side of the humanoid looking one: a ram and a bull. The blue of the seal clashed with the red and green flames that came off his body. Curling around his mismatched legs, his tail lashed out. I'd seen nothing so terrible in my life.

"You." The flaming eyes of his human head turned to me. Fur crawled up his cheeks and his lips were a cruel, sharp line. "Little human female. How could you summon me?" He drew closer to me and I think only the tightening horror of my core kept me from peeing in my summer shorts. "You cannot possibly possess this power. How did you manage it?" He sounded genuinely curious.

"I–I'm sorry," I managed. "I didn't mean to—"

He drew in through his nose. "Or maybe," he said, eyes narrowing at my new horns, "not so human after all. It takes the power of a god to bring me to the human realm. Who is your father, little one?"

"You owe us wishes!" Lizzy's thin voice rose behind him.

Asmoday's body turned in her direction.

"Lizzy, no!" I hissed. I needed to draw his attention back to me, so I yelped: "Veles!" Asmoday's three heads snapped back to me. "Veles is my father."

"Ah, the Slavic god of the Underworld," he said. "He has his seed walking on this earth. How resourceful of him. Or careless?" He stroked his chin, as if thinking about it. "Time will tell. Thank you for freeing me."

"Freeing?" Lizzy chirped. "You are ours to command!" She rose to all of her tiny frame. "I want—"

He silenced her with the wave of his hand. She clawed at her now mouthless face, eyes bulging in terror.

"Here's what no one tells you about summoning demons, little one," he said to me. "And the reason they don't tell you is because there are usually no survivors." His clawed hand pointed at the seal. "These seals do nothing to trap us. The summoner needs to have the power to contain us. Can you contain me, girl?"

Lizzy's round face was stricken. I reached my hands out to her, tears streaming.

"Run." I pushed at her. "Run!"

"You can't summon a Prince and not pay a price," Asmoday rumbled. "Today, it's not you paying it." Faster than I could blink, his giant claw plunged into Lizzy's chest. It pulled out something shining with a soft, effervescent light. Its shape was vaguely human. Lizzy collapsed onto the ground. I screamed as Asmoday shoved the shining essence into his mouth. The bull and the ram heads laughed as he sucked down Lizzy's soul. I was still screaming when he turned back to me.

"Until later, Veles' spawn." His eyes were amused. "I have a feeling you'll be useful to me again."

With a cloud of sulfur, he was gone.

The soul husk shimmered on top of Lizzy's body. It flapped like decaying plastic in the wind. I hadn't known what soul-dead meant back then. But I knew that my best friend was gone. Gone for good.

Back in the medical quarter, I pressed my palms to my eyes. Hot tears burned my eyelids. I pushed them back.

"You okay?" Henry's voice sounded over me. "I can give you something for the pain."

Shaking my head, I swallowed down the memories. There was nothing Henry could give me for shame and regret. "I'm good," I said.

He gave me a pitying smile. "Call me if you change your mind."

I nodded, and he packed up his kit. With a wink and a wave, he left me to my thoughts. My locker had my old hooded denim jacket. I threw it over my shoulders and zipped it closed.

When Rudy came back, I took the paper bag from his hands. It smelled like fries and jalapeño burgers. Biting into the stack of patties with cheese and a criminal amount of fresh jalapeños, I chewed before turning to the reaper.

"I don't think I can sit this one out," I said.

He raised his eyebrows, his pretty face unimpressed. "Shocking."

I chewed and swallowed. We weren't the ones that let out the devourers. Someone else had done it and made sure we got blamed. It wasn't just the demons. There were souls at risk, and they could use all the backup they could get. Stonefield didn't see it, but I did. And if I was careful, I wouldn't lose my badge. All I needed to do was to find information on where the demons were going and why they were really here. Astrid—and Hrom—didn't exactly know about all the unsavory sources of information one could find in a city overrun with demons. Luckily, I did.

"I'm only telling you, so you stay away from me for a while," I said to Rudy. "If I get caught, you won't be involved."

The reaper crossed his arms over his chest. "And you think that will keep me out of your business?"

"I think it will keep you out of trouble," I said.

"How long have we been riding together?" he asked.

I shrugged. "Almost a year?"

He nodded. "I don't like humans. You're messy and incompetent. It took me a while to get used to you, and I don't want another partner. If you're about to go poking around in this devourer business, you'll get caught."

"Rudy—"

"What's your plan?" he asked impatiently. "I know you have one."

The corners of my mouth lifted. "Yes, I do. I need to go shopping."

7

THE DEMON BAZAAR IS an entity all its own. Built hundreds of years ago, it was one of Hades' many micro-realms. The gods call these mini realms In-Betweens, their places between realities. Unfortunately, this one required an entry fee.

"We have to go to my mom's first," I said to Rudy. "We can't take the van, since we're suspended. Can you give me a ride?"

He side-eyed me from under his hood. "Don't you have a car?"

"But it's so much *slower*," I said. "I have to check on them, too." Now that the adrenaline was dying down, my anxiety found new purchase in my brain. "My mom is a whiz with wards, but even her Fae blood isn't strong enough to repel a devourer attack."

That much was true. She and her wife, Shelly, ran a crystal shop on King's Beach. It would take my car an hour to get there.

Giving me a long-suffering sigh, the reaper drew out his keys. "I suppose we better get this over with."

By time we got on I-80, the sun was pushing the day towards three o'clock. It was freezing atop the bike, and that was the only thing that gave away Rudy's nerves. So, I wasn't the only one who found the devourers taking the souls highly alarming. That made me feel better. The burger made an uncomfortable dance in my stomach as we shot through solid matter like it wasn't there. The gorgeous mountain range stretched under the sky as heat baked the desert. I felt pretty great until the reaper's bike sped up. Regretting asking for a ride, I hung on for my dear life. We rode through the trees and the hills, and patches of desert terrain. I didn't open my eyes until ten minutes later, when the bike slowed to something resembling a reasonable speed. We were rolling down a sandy road crowded by comfortable—and ridiculously expensive—pine wood cottages.

King's Beach—Kinky Beach to the locals—stretches across Lake Tahoe's north shore. Growing up there, I'd seen nomadic kids like myself, and the rich kids from Incline grow up the same way: wild. Just seeing the local businesses shaded in the trees lifted my spirits to something that resembled a dangerously good mood. Rudy parked on the side of the road next to a tiny, two-story building with a blue-tiled roof. The sign over the door read "Rainbow Road."

I took off my helmet and breathed in the clean, sharp air of Jeffrey pines. I smiled. Home, or at least as close as a nomad could have.

"I'll stay here," Rudy said. "Don't take too long."

"Or what?" I scoffed. "You'll go be insubordinate without me? I don't think so."

"I'll leave your half-human ass behind," he said evenly.

April isn't big on tourists, but mom's shop is always busy. And why not? Her crystals and remedies actually *work*. I walked under the sign and pushed the door open. The bell chimed. I knew every paint stroke of that sign. After all, I had painted it myself.

As I stepped through the door, essential oil and every incense known to man assaulted my senses. If there ever was a contradiction, it would be my childhood and my adult self. The little girl I used to be wouldn't stand for the way I was living my life now. The evenings spent alone. Working a straight job. Back then, it was unthinkable to me. I'd grown up in our wizard van. We sold crystals and teas out of the back.

My step mom was manning the register. She smiled at me over the heads of the regulars. A woman in her fifties with a broad, genuine smile, she had a pixie cut and two sleeves of mandala tattoos. She had the gently aging face of someone who was at peace with their crow's feet and their cushy middle. Mom had dated women for most of my life—my dad had been a weird exception—but no one made her want to settle down more than Shelly. Even when I was sixteen, I'd been glad for it. My life was quickly going down the rescuer route, and I had wanted to see my mom settled. Not to mention that "settling down" kept her somewhere I could keep an eye on her.

I waved at Shelly and blew her a kiss as she began ringing up another customer. She waved back.

"Mom?" I mouthed over the noise.

Shelly gestured toward the back of the shop. "She's beading with Amber."

No time for a family reunion. I left her to her work and walked through the store to the back. Sun hit my face as I stepped onto the gravel.

The two women crouching over a picnic table were putting shiny beads on silk strings. Multi-hued glass caught light and flecked color onto their faces.

Sarah May Green was still a wheat-haired beauty who could've given Stevie Nicks a run for her money. Her shawl covered her narrow shoulders. Her admittedly watered-down fairy blood gave her face an ageless grace. Amber was Shelly's daughter, who usually lived with her dad. Small and delicate, she sat cross-legged in her high-waisted jeans. The sight of them whispering enchantments over the crystal beads made my mouth soften. It was too easy to imagine myself in Amber's place. Carefree behind my mother's wards and my mother's love. I hadn't felt that safety in years.

"Chrys!" Amber sprang to her feet with the dexterity only accessible to teenagers and leprechauns. Her white teeth flashed and her shoulder-length hair haloed as she leapt toward me. She didn't give me a hug. At sixteen, she was too cool for sappy stuff like that. I grazed her knuckles with my own.

"Hey, dude."

My mom pulled me in. Smelling of rosemary, she held me in an embrace that felt like the sun. I let her examine me at arm's length. Her unsettling blue eyes, a copy of my own, always saw too much.

"Nathair bhig." I warmed at the sound of my mom's nickname for me. "Little snake" in Irish. Her fairy blood was thin, but the stamp of the Seelie Court was in her blue eyes that sparkled with unnerving emerald. "What's wrong?" she asked.

"There might be a minor problem," I said. Saying something like the demons have broken out of hell and I am being blamed for it, didn't sound right or very calming. "The Spiral is handling it, though. I just wanted to check in."

My mother didn't look convinced.

"Are you in some kind of trouble?" she asked. Internally, I swore at her perceptiveness.

"It's all going to be okay," I said. "There's been a demon outbreak—"

My mother gasped. "Chrys! Are you being safe?"

"They're not a high school boyfriend, mom," I teased. She wasn't impressed. I turned her away from Amber's sharp ears. "Is there somewhere you could go?" I dropped my voice. "Now? Shelly and Amber are humans, and shit's about to get real."

Any other mother would question this. However, my mom and I had been through too much. For most of my life, we'd been a team. She could read the urgency in my tone correctly.

"I could put them on a boat," she said quickly. "There is an old gentleman who has been begging to take us out on the lake for months."

Given my mother's charm, that wasn't surprising. "Perfect. How long can you stay on the water?"

Lake Tahoe wasn't always safe, of course. Lots of scary things lived in its depths. But most of them were ancient, and right now they were safer than the land.

"A few days," my mom hazarded. "How bad is it?"

"Perfect," I said, ignoring her question. "Close the shop and leave tonight." I tried for a smile. "It's just for a little while. It'll probably blow over soon."

She gave me a long look. Of course, she wasn't fooled.

"Take care of yourself," she said. "Promise me."

Licking my suddenly dry lips, I nodded. She knew about Lizzy, of course. After all, she was the one to rock me back to sleep after the nightmares that followed. That summer, she reached out to my father for aid. For most of my life, she had been the one to hide the harsh realities of the world from me. It was my turn to do the same for her.

"I need something from the van," I said.

Not questioning it, she grabbed the garage clicker from the shop. Gods eternal, I loved that woman.

I walked past the comfy trailer that my mom shared with Shelly and toward the garage. The garage had been built from a small shack that hailed from the 70s. It was fitting, seeing what it contained within. I pressed the clicker. Sunlight spilled into the stuffy space and sent the dust mites dancing. My mother's trailer was a testament to modernity. A new life she'd built with Shelly. But it wasn't the life I was born to. My home—my true home—was inside.

The van looked like something out of a hippie road trip movie. A purple coat was peeling on the forest of mushrooms and crystals that was both kitschy and meticulously painted by my teenage hand. Despite my current anxiety, a smile tugged at the corners of my mouth. We hadn't driven the Crystallizer in years, but I made sure it still ran. I climbed into the driver's seat. Upholstery cracked under my butt. I started the engine. Leaning my forehead against the dashboard, I listened to the ancient engine growl. The musty, fragrant air of my childhood rose around me. More than anything, I wanted to take it back on the road. To drive back in time, to when my life's purpose wasn't proving to myself that I wasn't a monster. But it wasn't the reason I'd come. I tapped the fuzzy polyester green that covered the dashboard and reached toward the glove compartment. Inside sat an old map of Reno. I pulled it out and slid it inside my jacket. The real treasure sat deeper inside. My fingers rummaged about until I felt cool metal. I pulled out a coin.

It was the size of a golden dollar, but it was *far* older. It was centuries older than the United States. A boat was imprinted into the metal and the edges were uneven. I had won this coin years ago from one of nymphs in Hades. I'd won five, actually. The times I'd used them to go to the Demon Bazaar weren't my favorite to remember. I kept the last coin as a souvenir. It wasn't exactly somewhere I should've been showing my face, but the demons there had something the Spiral didn't: information. Creatures, monsters, and half-bloods came and went from the Bazaar and rumors spread there quickly. If someone knew where the demons were heading, they would be there. I should be okay if I left quickly. Plus, it's been years since I'd been. I doubted there was someone still looking for me. Heart hammering, I slid the coin into my pocket. Climbing out, I patted the van's peeling paint.

"Let's all survive the day, buddy," I whispered. "Maybe I'll come back and take you for a drive."

As I closed the garage door, it felt like leaving a piece of myself behind.

Back in Reno, we left the Ducati in the parking lot of Circus Circus. Walking past the slot machines and chain-smoking seniors helped me snap out of my homesick melancholy. I had a job to do.

Rudy was riding in his usual broody silence and that suited me fine. I stopped at the descent to the underground tunnel that connected Circus Circus with its neighboring casino, Silver Legacy.

"You don't have to come with me," I said to him. "It might be dangerous. There are people at the Demon Bazaar," I waved downstairs, "that are *pretty* mad at me."

He gave me an even stare from under his hood. "Is there anyone who isn't?"

"They don't like the Spiral's lackeys there, either," I added. "No one's going to roll out the welcome wagon."

The skull flashed under the planes of his face. "I'm nobody's lackey," he said. "And we're not going to do anything illegal. We'll ask the questions and leave."

I didn't like how he made that a statement.

"Sure," I said too brightly.

"Then, I'm going," he shrugged. "Unless you only like me for my bike."

He began going down the stairs, leaving me to gape after him. Rudy *never* joked about the bike. Or *joked*, really.

"That's not true," I called, "I also like you for your ulaks."

My phone vibrated in my pocket. I pulled it out, expecting Chief Baran. The assigned profile picture in the middle of the screen was Popeye the Sailor Man. I frowned at the name it accompanied.

Zandro Hrom.

I stared at my phone in dumb incomprehension. Why the hell would the illustrious son of Perun be calling me now? For a second, I was tempted to answer. Then I pressed the red button with utmost satisfaction. I was sure *Astrid* could assist him with whatever he needed.

The escalators took us down into the underground passage. Sculpted sea creatures rose on either side as we rode the mechanism. Tritons, kelpies and cherubs were painted in green and gold as they spat water out of shells and ran above the cascading water. The kelpies had been real, once. These were the poor sods that were serving a sentence for drowning humans in Lake Tahoe and the Truckee River. Scratch the "poor" part, I suppose. We stepped off in front of a fancy restaurant. A pleasant—and bland—lounge music echoed off the sleek shining floors. We stepped down in front of the centerpiece—Fountain of Fortune. A self-important king of tritons rose twenty feet into the air while his marble subjects blew into conch shells.

The hostess of the restaurant—Roxy's—had a pair of adorable glamoured horns curling in her hair. She was *very* pretty, with pouty lips and wide-set eyes. A demon spawn, I guessed. Not that I knew what species. For a second, her eyes narrowed at the sight of me. Then she put her hands on her round hips.

"By whose invitation do you enter the Bazaar?" she demanded in a lilting accent.

"Charon's," I said and raised the gleaming coin.

"And him?"

"He's my bodyguard." I said in a stage whisper, "I'm very fragile."

Scowl deepening, she waved us to proceed. I tossed the coin into the fountain and stepped into the water. My Docs slurped. Rudy splashed in next to me and the magic, older than both of us, stretched down like a glistening whirlpool. We let the fountain take us.

8

THE WATER INSIDE WAS wet only for a second, and by the time the whirlpool spat us out, I felt wrung out like I'd been through the spin cycle. Nausea warmed up my throat.

We were standing somewhere in the Great Basin Desert. Or a version of it that Hades had seen centuries ago. The scent of desert rain and alkaline dust rose in the air. Distant thuds of house music pulsed through our bones. Rusty sand rippled under our feet and sagebrush covered the earth that led up to the sparkling lights of a city.

Demon Bazaar was a small area that stretched for several blocks. Around it, illegal supernaturals had built a nomadic town that could give Slab City a run for its money.

Tents, lean-tos, and ancient RVs dotted the desert. Generators rumbled between structures. There were fires and clusters of horned occupiers perched in front of fire pits. Sipping cheap beer in their camp chairs, they watched us as we passed. Hooved satyrs, mavkas, banshees, and others lived in uneasy peace that often erupted into violence. For them, it was preferable to their own pantheons. Many were on the run. Others liked the proximity to the human realm and its treasures. Every once in a while, a Spiral raid would trim down the city's population. It filled back up within a week. Rudy and I had our hoods up and we'd left our uniforms at home. People like Zan and his slayer bros gave us a bad name.

Most of the tents leading up to the neon streets of the Demon Bazaar were decorated with lights of their own. Tonight, the mood was friendly as the outcasts shared meals and stories over fires. Speakers boomed from Persian carpets. Giggles and conversation colored the night. Here, demon spawn ran free and were mostly protected from the world outside. It reminded me of the festivals my mom used to take me to. It seemed so far away now, and I felt like a different person. Still, the thrill of being here filled my bones. Shame wasn't the only reason I'd joined ERS. The fact was that I *liked* it. The danger, the hunt. And now, as we walked into the last place I should've been seen in Nevada, I felt that familiar thrill.

Rudy gave me a disapproving glare. "This place stinks of failure." Ulaks flashed at his belt. "Desperate creatures can be violent."

I gave Rudy what I hoped was a confident smile.

"We'll be fine," I said and nudged him. He looked at me like I'd slapped his ass. Honestly, I had no idea why the guy put up with me. "We just need to go see my contact. It'll be quick."

We walked into the market without an incident. I breathed in the scents. Fried meats of mysterious origins, cigars, weed, and deep-fried bread wafted over us. It was a hardy mixture of everything they sold and "didn't sell, thank you officer." Glowing signs and hand-drawn announcements lined the narrow street that haphazardly stretched between colorful shops. Displays with severed heads, dried herbs, and horn-enhancing potions overwhelmed us with their seedy offerings. The shops that were stacked on top of one another had narrow stairs leading to higher floors. Disco lights pulsed in time with the music as laughter and cloying perfume wafted out the windows. It wasn't the wares that were the most interesting. It was those who sold them.

Vodyanois, demons, fairies, and nymphs manned the stalls. Most of them didn't bother with a human disguise. In the human world, glamours hide gills, horns, and webbed fingers. Here they were on proud display. It was refreshing and a bit intimidating. I felt under my hood where my horns usually hid. Rudy and I were the most human-appearing in this lot.

I looked over my shoulders and kept my eyes and hair hidden under my hood. With any luck, we'd find the shop we were looking for and would be back in Reno in no time. Doing our best not to gawk around like a couple of tourists, we paused by the stalls and pretended to browse lizard claws and strings of black pearls. We were assured by a crawfish-faced kappa vendor these were made "in-house". I had to be discreet in wiping my hand. The market had changed in the two years since I'd last been, but I guided us past the bordellos and into the heart at its center. My shoulders tightened with nerves as we walked past the alley I was dreading. It was bathed in red light and smelled like cinnamon wine mixed with sweat. Incubus spice. Since I'm attracted to males, that's the thing I smelled first.

Inc and Suc is a demonic strip club. I'm still not sure how I'd ended up there in the first place. With the heady mixture of shame after the Hades incident, I didn't quite see straight back then. All I knew was that I had things to forget and the succubi were more than willing to assist. What followed was a six-month hedonistic tour that still had me waking up sticky with desire—and fear—in the middle of the night. Believe or not, the lust fest *wasn't* the naughtiest thing I did back then.

Whatever Rudy had smelled got his attention.

"What's down there?" he nodded toward the alley. There was a rare gleam in his eye. I never would've pegged the reaper for a thirsty boy. But then, Inc and Suc knew how to rile anyone's engine.

"Nothing interesting," I said. Grabbing him by the elbow, I nudged him along. "Just some folk you don't want to mess with."

His head turned as I dragged him past. He needed fresh air. Keeping my head low, I pushed on toward the glowing sign that said "Beasts and Books" in bold letters.

A green-skinned vodyanoi was manning the table. It was filled with cages and tattered scrolls. The water elemental hummed to himself. His seaweed hair was twisted into twin braids that hung behind his ears. A green beard covered his chin and his webbed hands were toying with a lock on a birdcage. Yellow canaries chirped from their perches and I smelled the dung and animal feed that permeated everything. I grinned at the sight of the pink apron stretched over his round stomach. His voice rumbled with an Old Slav accent as he nudged a pick into the opening.

"Give moment, young customer, and I will—"

With a casual movement, I leaned against the table.

"Hey, Step. How can a fish live in the desert?" I asked in Old Slav.

The vodyanoi perked up as if he couldn't believe his ears. Razor-sharp needles grinned at me and his yellow eyes lit up.

"He learns to breathe sand." He chuckled at our old joke. His arms went out. "Chrys!" I let the water spirit pull me into a cushy, moist hug. He smelled like seaweed and dog biscuits. "Good to see you!"

Stepan was a fugitive from Vyraj. "Expat" if you asked him. Ten years ago, he'd been chased out of his home pantheon by the other water spirits for breeding some kind of super-piranhas. Apparently, they destroyed a bunch of wildlife and went after the local rusalkas. Oops. You'd think he'd find a lake in Yav and take a wife, like any good vodyanoi. Instead, he took his talents to land. A few years ago, I'd rescued his niece from poachers, and we'd been friends since.

"You're looking well," I told him in English.

"Ah," he patted his stomach with a sheepish grin. "Soft life." He squinted at me. "I have not see you for long time. And I think this not for fun visit."

I unrolled a scroll on his counter and pretended to look inside.

"Nothing gets past you, Step," I said. "Can we talk somewhere more private?"

He nodded and gave a sharp whistle. A little green-skinned girl appeared from behind a row of cages. Her seaweed hair gave her away as a vodyanoi. Or a vodyanitsa, to use the proper term.

"Lena!" He pointed at the wares in front of him. "Watch counter." He walked toward a narrow door that led to the back portion of the shop. "My niece," he added at my questioning glance. "Here to learn trade in Yav."

I nodded. Vodyanois had extensive families that stretched across the world. Most of them preferred a quiet life in the water. Stepan was a bit of an anomaly.

"You coming?" Step inquired as he turned. "Honored guests are welcomed with drink."

Exchanging glances, Rudy and I followed him into the depths of the shop.

9

There was a table in the back of the shop with a few chairs. A single wilting lily sat in a vase in the middle.

"Sit, sit!" Step gestured toward the chairs. "I make drink." He disappeared toward what I assumed to be the kitchen. Clinking of dishes followed. The surrounding walls were filled with cages that barked, squeaked, and howled with various creatures. Some looked like birds but had eerily human faces, some resembled monkeys, but had bright-red limbs and breathed fire. The tanks were filled with creatures that only passed for regular sea life if you were drunk. Rudy's eyes went to a jellyfish that had thorns growing out its tendrils. It grabbed a pebble from the bottom of the tank and stuffed it into its mouth.

Rudy gave me a look of genuine incredulity.

"Wow," he said. "I don't think I've ever seen this many smuggling and illegal breeding violations all in one place."

I flicked the wilting lily.

"You should get out more."

"You have strange friends for someone who is supposed to be walking "straight and narrow."

I stared at him. "You're not responsible for me, you know that, right?" Leaning closer, I examined his closed-off expression. "You don't even like me."

His scowl deepened. "Is that what you think?"

I opened my mouth to answer, when a rumbling growl came from behind one of the cages. A three-headed dog leapt out. It was the size of a pit bull and its three jaws were open wide. Rudy's ulaks flashed in the corner of my eye. I raised a hand at the reaper. Three pink tongues lolled and three pairs of eyes burrowed into me with utter adoration.

"Hey, Bono!"

The dog wobbled up to me. Muzzles of each head nudged my hands to be the first one to get pets. I laughed as I scratched chins and rubbed foreheads. "Good boy." I looked at Rudy. "He's friendly."

The reaper slid his blades into their holster. "I can see that."

"Finally want to buy hellmutt?" Step asked as he walked back in with his arms full of steaming mugs. He balanced one of them on his stomach. "I can give you good price."

Hellmutts were distant relatives of hellhounds, the vicious soul trackers of Hell, and Cerberus. After hundreds of years of inbreeding, they resulted in three-headed lumps of adoration that could track anything in Yav. Supernatural bounty hunters used them. I kissed Bono on top of his middle head.

"Mittens would hate it," I said with a grin.

"Is shame." He placed two steaming mugs of green liquid in front of us. "Salamander Tail," he said. "House specialty."

I wondered how a smuggler-slash-breeder shop could have a house specialty, but decided not to question it. Rudy sniffed it with suspicion. I wasn't nearly as rude. Taking a sip, I felt my eyes water. I coughed, and the vodyanoi grinned.

"So, what you think?" Stepan's head fins flared.

Bono took a break from drooling onto my leather pants to look up at me expectantly. I smacked my lips. After the burn subsided, it wasn't half bad. The brew was slimy on the tongue, but the water lily aftertaste was pleasantly aromatic.

"Not bad," I said honestly. Rudy set the cup down without tasting it. Really, I couldn't take him anywhere.

The vodyanoi sat across from me. His smile slid off his face.

"What kind of trouble you in, eh?"

I tapped my glass. "Why is everyone asking that?" I said, "I'm not in trouble. Can't say the same about the state of Nevada."

"That devourer escape?" Step asked. That didn't surprise me. Gossip travels fast at the Demon Bazaar.

"Yes," I said. "It turns out they took human souls with them."

The vodyanoi hissed through his needle-point teeth. "Nasty business," he said. "Souls powerful fuel. If they took them, it is for reason." Grabbing a mister from under the table, he sprayed himself. He must be itchy in the dry Nevada air.

"Yes," I leaned back in my seat. "I need to find out where they're going."

He puffed his cheeks, which made him look like a green blowfish. "You need to let hunters do job," he said to me like he was my uncle. "It is dangerous to tangle with devourers."

"The hunters don't care about those souls." I didn't say Zan's name, which I applauded myself for. "I do. Do you know anything?"

Stepan took a long time to answer. "I owe you favor, I think." His fish eyes flicked at Rudy. "I don't know what I can do to repay." The message was obvious. Step was a friend, but he was also a wily old catfish. He knew something, but wasn't saying a word in front of an ERS operative he didn't share secrets with.

I looked at the reaper. "Hey, partner," I drawled.

He took a break from examining his ulaks for perfection. "What?"

"You look bored. Bet you'd find something illegal to get outraged about in the stalls next door." I raised my eyebrows at him. His eyes flicked to vodyanoi and back at me. He nodded. Rudy was many things, but he wasn't dense. His long legs swung out from under the table.

"I'll get some *fresh air*," he said.

With a clink of his weapons, he rose to his feet. The air around him was chilly when he left. I guess that's what happens when you're a literal personification of death. Bono whined, and I used two hands to scratch two heads. Cerberus blood inside the mutt could smell the reaper's death magic.

"Strange friend you have," Step said.

I shrugged. "He comes by it honestly."

"One reap souls and the other one eat them." Step grunted. He gulped his super-charged alcoholic sludge.

"We make it work," I said, as I eyed him. "What is it you don't want to tell me in front of Rudy?"

He looked uncomfortable and sprayed himself again. The last spritz went into his mouth and he cleared his throat. I waited. It was always better to bide your time when someone was unsure whether to tell you something.

"There was demon here late night," he said after a pause. "All twitchy like, as if someone was after him. Tick is his—her?—name."

I blinked. "His or hers?"

The vodyanoi waved a finned hand. "Hard tell, a boy or girl? When I ask, they said they are, ehh, 'an experience'."

I snorted into my drink. "I think this demon is non-binary, Step."

He looked at me blankly. "Is what?"

Tapping the table, I leaned closer and dropped my voice. "So what did they want?" I tried not to look too eager.

"Demon pop in now and then," Step said. "Scavenger. Interesting wares, find strange things. From Vegas area."

A smuggler and a thief from the great city of Las Vegas. Perfect.

"And yesterday? They brought something," I guessed.

"Tried to sell me soul husk," the vodyanoi said.

My shoulders stiffened. That made a grim kind of sense. Hellhounds ate soul husks to gain baffling amounts of power. So did hellmutts like Bono. It strengthened them. Seemed like this smuggler was smart enough to know to bring it here, and not try to sell it directly to a hellmutt owner, since most of them reported to the Spiral.

"Did you buy it?" I asked.

He threw up his hands. "Veles, no! Too nasty magic for Stepan." His double chin wobbled as he shuddered. "I didn't want anything to do with! Tick wanted to pay debt. I say no."

Taking my time, I thought about it. I didn't think he was lying, but I wasn't sure. I decided it wasn't likely. A thieving smuggler who just *happened* to be in a possession of a soul husk a day after a bunch of souls were stolen from Hell was too specific.

"Debt?" I asked.

Step scratched under his chin. "Tick me owes for item I... procure."

I tapped my boot as I thought about it.

"I'm calling in my favor, Step," I said. "I need to know how to find this Tick," I said.

The vodyanoi misted his round, glossy face with the spray bottle. I watched him over the rim of my cup. After a while, he deflated like a hot-air balloon. Honestly, by the standard of the Bazaar, I was letting him off easy. Whatever Tick owed him, it couldn't have been more than the life of his niece. In Step's mind, I could've asked for half of his shop. He didn't know that I would never demand anything of him. I didn't rescue people for cash. I crossed my legs at the ankles and did my best to look intimidating with a drooling dog on my lap.

To my relief, the vodyanoi took this easy way out of his "debt."

"I can't tell you where Tick is," he said. I opened my mouth to speak, and he waved his webbed palm, so I let him continue. "But I do have way to find out." His flat eyes met mine. "You will not like, I think."

He left and returned with a folded piece of paper. It was a lined sheet from a regular notebook. When he unfolded it, I grimaced.

Inside was a summoning circle. It was drawn crudely, like a child learning his letters.

"This Tick's seal," Step said.

Vodyanoi held it out for me. I hesitated before taking the vile thing. My fingers felt like I was touching something sticky as I turned it over. I hated summoning circles. Last time I used one, my childhood friend had lost her soul.

"It could summon anyone," I said. "They could've left you a dud. Or a trap." Lizzy's twelve-year-old face flashed in my memory. Screaming.

"I did warn that you won't like," he said.

I licked my lips, tasting water lilies. Then I took the seal and slid it inside my pocket.

"We are, how you say… 'Square' now?" he asked eagerly.

"Yeah, Step," I said, defeated. "We're 'square'."

This wasn't the answer I wanted, but that was hardly the vodyanoi's fault. I rose from my chair.

"Thanks for the drink," I told him.

Now that our business was done, Step looked much more relaxed. Or maybe it was his thousand-proof slime water. He smiled and downed his mug. Then he eyed mine.

"You will not finish it?"

"Next time maybe," I said. "Better find Rudy." I gave him a brief bow. "Thank you."

He grabbed my mug and saluted me. "Any time, Veles' daughter!" He chugged.

I went to the front of the shop where Lena was scribbling on a scroll with all the concentration of a straight-A student. Her braids were longer than Stepan's, falling down to her knees. Chubby green toes peeked out from under the hem of her dress. I couldn't help a smile.

"Hey kid. Did you see where my partner went?" I asked her. At her blank look, I clarified: "The cute guy that feels like standing next to a freezer?"

She nodded and pointed an ink-stained finger to the left of the stall.

"He said he smelled something," she said. Unlike her uncle's, her English was perfect. "Then, he took off."

"Smelled something?" I frowned. "Like what?"

She shrugged. "I dunno."

I looked up and down the street, but couldn't see my partner over the heads of the milling Bazaar customers. Smelled something... That didn't bode well.

A wet nose nudged my hand, and I looked down to see Bono. His three pairs of eyes stared up at me. I brushed the top of his heads.

"Say, Bono," my eyes darted down the street. "Think you can sniff out Rudy for me?"

I patted my pockets and found Rudy's bike gloves he'd let me borrow.

"Here," I put them under his muzzles. Three noses breathed in the scent and sneezed, one after the other. Then, the hellmutt started down the street. I was willing to bet that if he'd known Rudy's name, I wouldn't even have had to bother with the gloves. All he would have to do is follow the smell of death.

Waving goodbye to Lena, I went after him.

A weird purplish smoke rolled down the street, curling on the dark brown sand of the Nevada desert. It smelled a bit incensy. People passed me without noting anything strange. I didn't like the way their eyes went over my head.

"Rudy?" I called.

Reaper or not, Rudy wasn't immortal. His soul was bonded to the Christian Yawei for sins he committed on earth. He was damn hard to kill, but I didn't know anyone who wouldn't go down with a well-placed bullet to the head.

The purple smoke circled up my boots and crawled up my jeans. I could feel its sticky curls on my skin. This felt distinctly like a demonic trap. A succubus trap, to be exact.

My suspicions were confirmed when we turned the corner and ran into the last place I wanted to be.

Red light radiated from the windows. Half of them were shuttered, but there was one beacon of disco lights that pulsed out onto the street.

That's where Rudy's ass had wandered off to. Inc and Suc.

10

THERE IS NO "GUNS blazing" when it comes to succubi. I pulled down my hood and zipped the front of the hoodie up to my nose. It wouldn't do much to fight the pheromones, but, luckily, they were the wrong kind to entice me. These pheromones were distinctly cis female. Not my cup of tea. Although, they were clearly Rudy's. I fell into the shadow of a building and considered my options.

I had my gun and not much else. If I'd driven my van here, I could just bust through the frontage of the strip club and grab my partner. He wouldn't be happy, but a snare of perfect succubi tits wouldn't enslave him. And they were *perfect*. I've seen them up close, almost gave me a complex. I couldn't call it in. Cell phones didn't work at the Bazaar. In-Betweens are on a separate layer of reality from the human world. No cell towers to speak of. By the time I got back to Reno to find help, it would be too late for Rudy. He'd be as good as enslaved by the lust demons for who knows how long. Lafayette had almost gotten me for a lifetime. Incubus venom didn't play games.

Lafayette... Calling him my "ex-boyfriend" didn't quite sit well. A "boyfriend" hinted at something romantic. Something cute. There was nothing "cute" about Lafayette and I. I had been desperate and he'd been willing to take advantage of that. We should've had our fun and gone our separate ways. Except that I did what I do best—royally piss demons off. But it's been two years. How long could a guy hold a grudge?

The succubi trapped a person using their own lust. Rudy being a horny boy was the last thing I expected. I shouldn't have let him go off on his own.

A sound of pitter-patter came toward me from the street.

"Go home, Bono," I whispered to the hellmutt. "Go back to Step. It's not safe here."

He whined and trotted past to the back of the building. Throwing a glance over my shoulder, I swore and followed. He must've been still tracking Rudy, but at least he wasn't marching us down the main street for everyone to see.

Tongues lolling out of three jaws, the pooch led me down a back alley. I tried not to look too closely at the debris at my feet. Something slurped under my boot and I shuddered. Bordello trash, that's just what I needed.

We took a turn and walked under a line of tattered laundry. Bono stopped and whined up at the open window above. Some techno beat spilled from it and I could see the lights pulsing with the music. A familiar smell hit my nostrils. Those cis female pheromones. We were at the back end of Inc and Suc.

"Good dog!" I said to Bono. He gave me a triple dose of the adorable doggie smile.

I climbed up some crates and drew out my salt gun. Peering inside, I squinted against the dark.

Pink lanterns hanging off the roof were shaped like dancing women with round hips and leering smiles. This looked like the room where the *real* party took place. My eyes followed a trail of glittering bras and panties up and down couches that were wide enough to be used as beds.

Rudy was sitting on a chair in the middle of the room. A succubus straddled his lap. She wore a bikini so small I didn't know why she bothered. Her tail swooshed back and forth on the floor to the beat of the music. Had Rudy walked back there of his own accord? The reaper didn't seem to be bound by anything but the double D cleavage swinging in front of his face. I cocked an eyebrow. The girls at the office often gossiped about the handsome reaper and about his insistence on only working with me. The other squads were firmly jealous, which made the rumors spread. This proved that Rudy didn't start working with me because of my "rocking hot bod," or whatever. Between trekking through the Underworlds and chugging Red Bull instead of meals, my boob size was "D minus."

Another succubus was leaning on her elbows and facing the door. She looked intent, every curve of her ridiculously seductive body tight with anticipation. Her horns twisted around her ears. Unlike mine, they resembled a ram more than a goat. I imagined myself wearing that string bikini get up and almost laughed out loud. I could maybe pull off the heels. I checked the level of salt in my gun and weighed my options. Smashing through and taking Rudy seemed like my best option. Getting out of the Bazaar unscathed was a little more complicated. Rudy's face told me he was almost a goner. We'd cross the escaping bridge once we got to it.

Not wasting any time, I kicked my boot through the window. Surprise, ladies!

The succubus smashing her boobs into Rudy's face yipped. I swung my legs through the frame and landed in a crouch. Her long legs whipped around as she did one of those complicated somersault things off Rudy's lap. And they say strippers aren't athletes.

Riding the element of surprise, I gave the succubus a warning shot. With my fist. She staggered back, clutching her pretty face.

Rudy's cheeks were flushed as he gaped at me. That had me all kinds of worried. Who knows what happened when you drank a reaper's sexual energy?

The succubus chick recovered quickly. Her long tail whooshed over my head. I ducked and countered with a quick punch to the stomach. The second succubus lunged at me with her claws, and I dodged to the side. Firing my salt gun, I shot the "lady of the night" right in her boobs. She cried out in pain as the salt burned her skin. No chain mail bikinis for her for a few days. I delivered a series of rapid punches. It wasn't enough to kill her, but enough to make her double over in pain. With her head down, I delivered a quick kick to her temple, just like the Chief Baran taught me years ago. She dropped unconscious.

The first succubus recovered and grabbed a whip from the table. She swung it at me, but I was ready for her. I dodged the knotted leather cable. It snapped over my head like a gunshot. I've been to Lilith's realm enough times to know what being whipped with one felt like. Pain is the best teacher. No way was she getting me. I used her own momentum as she expected the blow to land to get inside her guard. Honestly, comic book writers everywhere should re-think chain mail bikinis. I punched her right in the mesh. She hissed. Her teeth were straight and beautiful, unlike most demons from her pantheon. The seductress lost most of her seductive mojo as the chain mail dug into her skin. I oophed as I realized, too late, the error of my ways. She might've gotten one hell of a bruise, but my hand stung like I'd broken my knuckles. The succubus stared at me like she couldn't believe I went after her *precious.* Her tail whipped around to knock me off my feet. Not wasting time, I put my boot to her temple in a 90-degree kick. She dropped beside her friend.

Unsteadily, Rudy rose to his feet. With his hood down, his blond hair was artfully tussled. He looked like he'd just stepped outside a club for a smoke. He pulled out his twin ulaks and stared at the succubi at his feet.

Wiping a scratch on my cheek, I winced in pain.

"You're just a smidgeon late," I said. "All the wicked ladies are down."

His eyes went to the fallen succubi that somehow still managed to look sexy passed out. The music thumping from the front room of the club had effectively smothered all sounds of battle. He looked so genuinely bewildered, I laughed.

"I was just about to handle it." He put away his weapons and pulled up his hood.

"You were about to handle *something*," I said smugly.

To my glee, Rudy colored again. I wished I was recording this.

"I don't know how—" He stopped. "How did I get here?"

"Giant boobs, apparently," I said brightly. "And succubus pheromones." Yes, I wasn't above needling him. "Time to get out of here before more strippers show up to kick our ass."

Rudy huffed, and I grinned.

He flicked the glitter off his shoulder. "Let's just forget this happe—"

A slow clapping came from behind a shimmering beads curtain.

I stopped dead in my tracks as I saw a shadow fall across one of the unconscious succubi bodies. A scent pierced through the thick perfume pheromone cloud that seemed to be beating into me with every thud of the stripper music. It replaced the female pheromones with something else. Something distinctly male and *so* seductive. *My* kind of seductive.

"Oh, Chryssy."

The sexiest baritone I've ever heard in my life caressed my spine.

"I *missed* you," the voice breathed.

Rudy froze, his eyes snapping over my head to the man standing behind me. That's when I realized that the trap laid out by the succubi wasn't for Rudy.

It was for me, after all.

I didn't hesitate. Spinning around, I shot a round of rock salt straight at the newcomer.

Except he was no longer there. I heard a crack and Rudy's surprised grunt. Whipping around, I saw the reaper's form rippling from solid to incorporeal. Rudy's ulaks were drawn, but useless, because he wasn't really *there* anymore.

"You were invited here with Charon's coin, but I am a master of this place." The sexy baritone came from my right. He sounded bored. "You are hereby *uninvited*."

"No!" I grabbed for Rudy, but there was no stopping the spell. His eyes wide, the reaper ceased to exist at the Demon Bazaar as the In-Between kicked him out. I wasn't sure where he went. It could've been Reno, or maybe the Universe sent him somewhere she thought he belonged. Like Purgatory. Or Hell. Wherever he went, it wasn't a place he'd get back from quickly enough to help me.

I was alone in the room with the master of Inc and Suc and, by extent, all the succubi of the Demon Bazaar. I turned toward him, my gun feeling utterly useless in my hand as his pheromones started working their way into my brain.

"Lafayette," I breathed.

11

IF THE SUCCUBI WERE sexy in an over-the-top, blow-up doll kind of way, the man standing in front of me was sex itself. He was just under six feet tall and bare chested. His muscles were gently pronounced under his glistening skin. He moved with the gorgeous dexterity of a dancer. Or a predator. His face had a long chin, a prominent nose, and eyes so amber they looked ready to set the surrounding couches on fire. Nothing could compete with his smile, though. It could melt the panties off a snowman. A pair of twisted ram horns curled up and behind his ears. Just the sight of them made my head itch. When we'd been together, I never put away my horns. Making love to Lafayette in my true form had been a new level of release. I blinked at the direction my thoughts had pivoted. Rudy was gone, and I was in deep shit. When had I started thinking about sex?

I lifted my gun higher and aimed at his smirk.

"How did you know I was here?" I asked.

"Oh, baby," his voice turned pitying. "How could I ever stop waiting for you?"

Licking my lips, I stood my ground. My salt gun trembled.

"You haven't seen me in two years. There's no way you could've known I came today. There's a ton of people coming and going, at all hours." Not even Step knew I was coming.

He began walking toward me. "I knew you were coming the second you stepped into that fountain."

"How—" I tore my eyes away from his sculpted torso and wrestled with my thoughts. "Oh. The hostess at the restaurant. She was a succubus."

"Half-succubus," he corrected me. Spreading out his arms, he inclined his head and tsked. "Please don't resist me. You know it hurts my feelings."

My breath caught as he stepped toward me. His body was unnaturally fluid, but that's what happened when your entire being—your purpose—was wired in seduction. Hell, two years ago, I'd fallen for it. And *how*. Except the way he was looking at me today was different. Back then, I was an exciting new toy. Someone he wanted to please as long as I pleased him in return. Now, he looked at me like I was a toy he wanted to break.

"Robbed any demons lately?" His smile was sexy, but it wasn't kind. "Who am I kidding? Of course you have."

He leapt at me faster than I could react. My gun clattered to the floor. His arms wrapped around me and the full force of his pheromones hit my senses. I thrashed, but we both knew it was too late. Heat traveled from my stomach into my groin. His palm brushed my cheek and cupped the back of my head. He leaned down and ran his tongue over my lower lip.

Incubus venom hit my core. Suddenly, all I wanted to do was to kiss him. Drink him in through his mouth before I stamped my lips down his neck. My bones ached with the desire to run my fingers through his hair and disappear into the ember flames dancing in his eyes. The top of my head burned as my horns made their appearance.

Recognition lit his lovely face. And it was lovely. I'd forgotten how his cheekbones stretched down to his mobile mouth like the dune ridges of his home underworld.

"Oh. I've missed you," he cooed. His expression didn't quite match his voice or the way his body was responding to the way he was holding me. There was anger there. "I never stopped waiting for you."

Missed my energy, you mean. A distant jolt of reason struck my brain. Unfortunately, it didn't make it down to my loins. Right now, all I wanted to do was be wanted. I've been alone for so long. I've missed being wanted.

His arm went around my waist. "How long would it take you to pay off the people you stole from me? How many were there, 5?"

6 and you were sucking them dry, you asshole. Again, the voice of reason didn't stop me from rubbing my thigh against his crotch.

"Maybe a year," he cupped my cheek. "Or five?" His hand cupped my breast and his finger ran over my nipple. I was ready to give him twenty. Anything for him to keep touching me.

I took six people out of Inc and Suc that were being tapped for sexual energy, which had been used to power the lust demons. Some of them had come willingly. Others owed favors. The day I broke them out to the human world, I didn't care. By the unspoken rules of the Demon Bazaar, Lafayette was right. I owed him years of servitude for the energy I had stolen. An incubus could feed on a human for weeks before they had nothing else to give. A demigoddess? The energy he could suck from me would fill metaphorical coffers.

His hands ran down my thighs, and all shreds of reason fled me.

"We'll play it by ear," he sighed.

"Let me go..." I whispered. My gun was somewhere on the floor, covered in stripper glitter. I couldn't quite get the words out of my mouth. Past mistakes notwithstanding, the last thing I wanted was to be back where I was two years ago. It would be worse now. Back then, I had wanted to forget, wanted to let my fear and guilt dissolve in the waves of sex and incubus venom. I had wanted the techno music and tangled sheets to replace the pockets in my brain that screamed that I was evil, a soul-sucking monster. Instead of being one, I gave myself to one.

"I have to... save them," I said through the cotton balls in my mouth. "Please. The souls. No... Time."

"Oh," he pressed his lips to my temple, "the souls the devourers took? Is that why you're here?" His laughter rumbled through his chest. "We know their master well. After all, he is our kinsman."

My thoughts smooshed into each other as I blinked up at him. "Their master is an incubus?"

"Don't worry about that," he said. "Don't you worry about anything anymore. You're back and that's all that matters. Let me take you. All of you."

I wanted him to take me. I was ready.

Lafayette's hands brushed up my thighs and cupped my buttocks. What was left of reason left me. I ground my hips to the swelling at his crotch. The song in my chest quieted and the gem at my wrist dimmed its blue glow in response to lust magic. That was one problem with being the daughter of the god of cattle—you knew exactly how babies were made. Electricity made my hair stand on end as my hand flattened against his smooth stomach and slid down.

Wait. A thought sludged through my lust-addled brain. Electricity?

Lafayette's eyes barely had time to widen before he was blasted away from me. His body slammed into the wall like he was a dead carp. He twitched. I blinked in confusion. Had Rudy found his way back somehow? And developed the powers of the electric chair?

Without the incubus supporting me, my knees gave.

An arm thicker than my thigh caught my waist. A muscled chest cushioned my shoulder blades. I looked up to see a scruffy jawline with a prominent dimple. The scent of rain and smoke enveloped me.

Zan, the son of Perun, hauled me up to my feet. His eyes were trained on the incubus stirring to life.

"You're dead, demon," he said. His voice vibrated through my core. Unlike Lafayette's, it broke through the spiderwebs. Not weaved them. "How dare you touch her without permission?"

I tittered up at him. "You smell *good*."

Ignoring me, he thrust his free arm to the side. A glint of metal caught the light of the pink lamps. Perun's axe looked as out of place in a bordello as Zan himself.

Lightning swirled around us. Left hand supporting me, Zan's right flicked out and I could feel the current go up my hair.

"I'll send you back to Lilith," Zan said.

My hand shot out to his forearm. Damn, his muscles felt good under my touch.

"Wait—" I searched for words that wouldn't count as sexual harassment. They were hard to find. "He—controls this part of the Bazaar. If he dies, there will be a fight for power. Huge fight." I swallowed. "Casualties."

A million years seemed to pass before Zan lowered his axe.

"Fine," he said. I saw him eye the incubus with loathing in his eyes. I wasn't entirely sure why he wanted to kill him so much. Couldn't have been because he was jealous. The son of Perun despised me. He'd made that clear years ago. "I hate it when you're right."

The sound of music halted. There were alarmed voices and the sound of whips cracking in the air.

"Reinforcements," I managed.

My eyes went to my infiltration route, and I almost laughed. Imagining Zan trying to squeeze through the narrow window was almost worth the amount of trouble I was in. The fact that we were trapped seemed to occur to him as well. He was good at killing demons, but subduing them required a subtlety that he lacked. I heard him swear in Old Slav. Something about slutty lizards. I think.

"Climb onto my back," he said. He rolled his shoulder for emphasis. I had to catch him around the waist to keep on my feet. Incubus venom roaring in my ears, I had to bite my lip to keep a school girl giggle from slipping out. Getting to wrap my legs around his waist? Someone twist my arm.

Achy and breathless, I wrapped my arms around his neck and drew my legs up to circle his butt.

"Wait!" I gasped. "My gun." I pointed until he spotted it on the floor.

With impressive accuracy, he kicked it out of the glitter and plastic beads and up to his waiting hand. He shoved it into his pocket.

I smelled his sweat through the cotton shirt that stretched over his back. It smelled amazing. His hair was pulled up into a short ponytail. A rebellious lock had escaped and curled at the nape of his neck. I wanted to twist it around my finger.

Feathers sprouted under me as hard muscles turned to tawny blades of feathers. Zan's body expanded, and I yelped before adjusting my grip. The stripper dance floor disappeared beneath me as he changed into a giant eagle. I screamed as his powerful legs pushed off that filthy floor. With a crunch, the flimsy ceiling caved in. Bits of cement and roof tile showered over my head. Dust blocked my airways.

Above us, the star-dotted sky opened up like an embrace. We were flying.

12

THE FEATHERS WERE SLEEK on top and soft as dandelion puff on the bottom. I buried my face into the fluff and felt the rush of adrenaline take my addled brain to really fun places.

Strong wing muscles pumped us up higher and higher. I flattened myself against his back and hung on for dear life. My heart was beating out of my chest. Is this what it felt like to ride a roller coaster drunk?

The twinkling lights of the city beneath were replaced by shrubby vegetation and tumbleweeds. Suddenly, it wasn't so fun anymore. It didn't take me long to slip. I screamed as a pocket of air pushed me to the side. Grabbing on for dear life, I pulled out handfuls of feathers. The eagle screeched as my feet kicked his sides. Incubus venom made you weak in the knees. Literally. The sky and the ground went topsy-turvy. With a scream, I slid off the sleek feathers and plummeted into the dark.

Wind pushed me from all sides and I gasped for air that wouldn't fill my lungs. Gravity shoved me toward the earth, and the quickly approaching landscape that only a jackrabbit could love. I wondered if Rudy would come to collect my soul. Somehow, I thought if he did, the reaper would laugh all the way to Veles's Underworld. What happened when demis died and went home to their pantheons? I guess I was about to find out.

The feeling of terrifying weightlessness stopped suddenly as a claw grabbed my ankle. Something cracked deep within my spine. Looking towards my feet, I watched as the giant eagle spread his wings. His silhouette was dark against the stars. I heard a deafening screech ring overhead. I expected us to go up, but instead we slid down. The eagle went with the wind instead of against it. I felt like a chicken strung up on a wire as we sailed toward the ground.

I was still a good two feet in the air when my foot slipped out of my boot. With a cry, I plummeted. My shoulder hit the ground, and I rolled, flattening a whole grove of creosote bushes. The scent of desert rain rose around me in an aromatic cloud. I stopped when the side of my head met a rock. My horns protected my temple. I'd forgotten they were there.

"Oowweee," I moaned, my hands pressing my forehead. Pain pulsed to the back of my teeth. The shrubs doubled in my vision. Curling up into myself, I counted my limbs. The right side of my head was splitting pain. My right eye's vision darkened as I touched my forehead.

"Shit," I murmured. Instead of the pointy end of my horn, I found a stub. Great, now I was looking like Hellboy.

I smelled pine and rain as a shadow blocked the sky.

"Shit!" Zan echoed my sentiment as he fell to his knees over me. I decided that I liked him on his knees. "Chrys, you okay?"

"Peachy," I moaned.

"Come on," he whispered. He tucked something under his arm. "I got your boot."

His hands went under my armpits, and my vision blinked out.

Next thing I knew I was wrapped in a leather jacket that smelled like rain. My head felt like my skull was split in half. I opened my mouth to say something cohesive. Instead, I babbled like a drunkard.

"Shh..." he said. "Almost there."

His hand went into his pocket, and he clicked a key fob. A flash of lights answered up ahead.

"You..." I croaked. "Drove?"

Who takes his Jeep to the Demon Bazaar in another dimension?

He grinned. "The Bazaar isn't technically a demon realm, so I have access anytime. No treaty breaking necessary."

Zan was Perun's heir and a seriously overpowered guy. Technically, he could break into almost any pantheon. That's why they kept such good tabs on his access.

"Bra-" I swallowed. My head pounded, and I had a hard time seeing out of my right eye. "Braggart."

He opened the backdoor and slid me in onto leather seats that smelled like citrusy spice.

"You hit your head pretty hard," he said. "Here." He leaned over me and turned on the cabin lights. "Let me see."

His giant frame crowded the already ridiculously spacious backseat. I could feel the heat of him through the jacket he'd carried me in. Hovering over me, his face was suddenly strikingly familiar. My vision span from pain. The slope of his cheekbones and his wide jaw framed the rest of the features of his face. Lips that weren't any sort of lush or pouty had a sharply defined bow. Everything was well balanced on his face. Unlike me, I never remembered him being an awkward adolescent. A burst of desire warmed my stomach. He was just so damn beautiful. Beautiful and full of edges. Like his axe. Even when he wasn't a man yet, he'd already looked like one. This position we were in was familiar, too. His breath, so close. His heat radiating all the way through to my bones.

Incubus venom roared in my blood. My hand grabbed the back of his head and I pulled him down to my mouth. His eyes widened as my tongue did a languorous circle around his. Then they fluttered closed and his lips answered with surprising urgency.

When we were teenagers, he didn't have monster tattoos yet. They would come later, as his father, Perun, rewarded him with one for every monster he'd slayed. His arms had been bare, and his face beardless when he had hovered over me, just like he was doing now. We'd started dating in Camp Demi, a camp for demigod and creature teens, to further their supernatural education.

After I met Zan, I began furthering my education alright. I'd been afraid to tell him who I was, of course. I knew there was weird beef between my father and his. The twins, Jaro and Rad, never stopped talking about their illustrious father or how Zan was going to pick up his mantle someday. They also told me about his mortal enemy, the dragon god Veles. I stayed quiet through these lectures. I'd learned my lesson about exposing my true nature in that hut the night Asmoday killed Lizzy. Brushing off the tales as superstitious Old World nonsense, I dove into the romance with Zan with all the vigor of a besotted seventeen-year-old.

On the night he broke my heart, we'd sneaked into one of the abandoned cabins in Camp Demi. My legs were wrapped around his hips, and my breath was hitched at the back of my throat.

"Is this okay?" he'd whispered to me.

We had been lying on the lower mattress of a bunk bed. My body was like a drawn bowstring, trembling with readiness. Taut with desire. I had barely known what desire was back then. Proximity and clean mountain air made the camp flings burn hot. Our romance was like a forest fire, an explosion. A super volcano. I remember the feeling of my hitched skirt pressing around my hips. I could see silver flashing in his dilated pupils. What had led to that night was three weeks of make-outs in broom closets, late in the cafeteria, and in the back of an empty bus. His thumbs hooked around the sides of my panties.

"Chrys?"

I nodded. I didn't have the words for the way my head had been swimming. He hadn't been the first boy I'd kissed. But he had been the first one who made me want to do more. "Yes," I whispered finally. His smile was wicked as he looked down at me. The weight of his body lifted and slid down as his lips trailed down my stomach.

"What—" my breath caught. "What are you doing?"

I could feel his mouth stretch into a smile against my skin. "I'm a gentleman," he'd whispered, voice muffled. "I think."

I gasped at what he did next. It was burned into my consciousness like a fire-hot brand touching leather. The pleasure had built in me like a starburst. It was so sharp that it almost hurt. It rolled up my body like a wave of prickling heat.

Then pleasure turned to agony.

Pain erupted from my forehead and I bucked, making Zan slam his head into the bed above us. I screamed. My horns split through my skin all at once. No warning. Terror replaced lust like a shot to the head. I gasped, my hands going up to the sudden new addition to my skull. I hadn't felt them come since the night I'd summoned Asmoday. Zan fell away from me, horror on his face matching my own.

"What is it?" he'd asked over my shrieks. "What did I do?" He reached out his hands. "Let me see."

Sobbing, I did. The look on his face was the one I'd never forget.

Stricken and wide, his eyes went dark with suspicion.

"What are you?" he said. "I thought you said you were a nymph?"

"I lied," I said meekly.

"Are you a demon spawn?" he asked.

"No!" I protested. "I-I'm..." I sat up on the bed, my face flushing in shame. I pulled my skirt down over my knees. "I'm Veles' daughter."

Zan froze. He looked like I just told him I'd crawled from the pits of Hell. Actually, he looked like he would've preferred that to the truth. "V-Veles?"

I nodded, feeling suddenly cold in the night. My sweat was beginning to dry on my body.

He was visibly pale now. Moving as if he was trying his best not to run, Zan stumbled out of the cabin. My heart thumped against my chest, breaking. Watching him go had realized my worst fears—everyone thought I was a monster, even Zan.

The next day, I packed my bags and called my mom. I still remembered standing in that summer breeze, my long boho skirt dancing around my ankles. My eyes were trained on the road where I'd waited for her wizard van. I wouldn't cry, I refused. Later, Rad told me that Zandro had looked for me, wanting to explain, but I didn't care. I was done with people looking at me like I was a monster.

The realization that I was kissing him brought me back to the present. I broke away, panting.

"Chrys?" His lips were puffy from the kiss, and his eyes were filled with concern, not revulsion. "What was that? Are you okay?"

I blinked up at his five o'clock shadow. His fingers gingerly touched my broken horn. He winced in sympathy.

"I think so," I said. I wasn't feeling so well. What had I done? From that moment in the cabin, when I wanted a boy so badly it triggered my goddess power, he'd seen me as nothing more than the daughter of his father's enemy. "Never mind."

"But you—" Zan said.

Reality shifted, and my eyes began rolling into the back of my head.

"Chrys?" Zan called over the sickening wave. His voice sounded distant. There was a tapping of hands on my cheeks. "Hey!"

If I only had a concussion, I had my demi blood to thank for it. A human would probably be dead. I felt nausea roll up my throat and my vision darkened.

What I remember next was the door slamming shut on the passenger side and Zan yelling something into his cellphone in Old Slav. The Jeep rolled uphill, and I'd lost whatever grip on reality I still had.

13

I WOKE TO THE sounds of birds making a fuss outside the window. The pillow under my head was the cushiest thing ever felt in my life. I was groggy, and still tired to the core of my bones. But there was a warmth and lightheadedness that felt like I was finally over a bad flu. The air smelled unfamiliar, like pine and wood smoke and frying bread. This is when I knew that I wasn't at home. No one made me pancakes in the morning.

When I opened my eyes, I saw sunshine dotting the lush carpet spread out the floor. I was lying on king-sized bed. That made a jolt of panic shoot through me for a moment. I checked my clothes to make sure they were intact, like a girl after a frat party. My jeans were still on, but someone had changed me into a soft cotton T-shirt that was far too long on me. A man's shirt with an ERS logo on it. I was barefoot. The rest of the giant bed didn't look disturbed.

I lifted my head and groaned. My right horn throbbed with tear-jerking pain. The memory of last night came to me in bits and pieces. Me falling right into Lafayette's trap. Rudy being uninvited from the demon Bazaar. And then… Zan. Zan? He saved me. The memory of the fall resurfaced, too. And then the car. Ooph. The *kiss*. I shuddered a bit with the aftermath of wanting Zan so badly, it triggered the last thing I wanted to remember about him. The clock over the bed showed ten o'clock in the morning. The souls. How much time had I lost? Rudy had—

Rudy!

I grabbed the phone off the nightstand. I still had half the battery left. That was the good news. The bad news was that I still didn't have a signal. I smacked the side of my Samsung to no effect, then stuffed it into my pocket. I needed to find a better spot.

I swung my legs out of bed.

"Yeep!" a tiny voice erupted from under my feet. I jerked my feet off the ground. My heart pounding, I lowered my head to look at the foot of the bed.

A pair of giant yellow eyes stared up at me, and a tiny mouth scowled. The woman was about two feet tall and her hawkish nose was stained with soot. She'd gathered her hair up into a messy bun. A house spirit of some sort, I guessed. Like a brownie. I squinted at her as my summers in Vyraj gave me context.

"A domovoi?"

The woman scoffed. "A kikimora!" She corrected me indignantly. "Do I look like a man to you?"

My eyes went from her to the window that opened onto the view over a lush green mountain. I recognized the Nevada Sierras, so we were still in Yav. Only Slavs had domovois to care for their homes. Or kikimoras, if they were ladies. The events of last night made my location obvious.

I asked anyway. "Where am I?"

The house spirit cocked her head and she wiped her hands on her apron. "You are in Eagle Nest, of course. Master Zandro brought you here last night." Her voice carried indulgent tolerance, like Zan had brought home another stray. "We have been caring for you, the house spirits of Eagle Nest." This is when I saw the tray that I had almost lowered my foot into. It had a pot of tea with a flowery bird design and a jar of painkillers. The kikimora sniffed.

"Master Zan is waiting for you downstairs, honored guest."

With a pop, she disappeared into thin air. I frowned at the spot where she used to be. Zan. This was his fancy home and his house spirit. Not too shabby, son of Perun.

Lowering my feet onto the patterned carpet, I picked up the tray and placed it on the nightstand. I took a better look around the room. A carved oak vanity showed me the last thing I wanted to see—my own reflection.

My forehead was purple on the right side. The glossy black curve of my horn was now a broken stump. I touched it and winced. At least it matched the dark circles under my eyes. The bruise began to spread down from my temple to my cheekbone. It promised to be a bona fide shiner tomorrow. Super.

Walking from one corner of the room to the next, I looked for a signal again. No dice.

"Please be okay," I whispered. Rudy was a big boy and could take his pound of flesh. Hopefully, he was in Reno, fuming as he tried to get back into the Bazaar, and not in the ninth circle running from hellhounds.

I staggered into the bathroom. An onyx bathtub straight out of a Fancy Homes magazine took up most of the space. It pictured fire birds of Slavic legend flying through delicate forests of stone. Its smooth, multi-hued surface was begging me to open the faucet and climb inside. The air smelled like expensive lavender soap. I stopped in front of the matching sink, turned on the faucet, and splashed my face. I wanted to brush my teeth and no sooner than I thought that, a travel pack caught my eye. It looked like Zan was running a fancy hotel.

Feeling a bit more refreshed, I went back into the bedroom. I drank the tea and swallowed the pills. I wasn't sure how much Ibuprofen would help, but it was worth a shot. The smell of frying eggs, onions, and bacon wafted from somewhere below. My stomach lurched. Laughter and conversation trickled up the stairs. I paused, unsure of what to do. Then, I decided that after a day like yesterday, I didn't give a shit about who saw me with my horns out and looking like death. A winding staircase took me to the lower floor, and I stepped onto a bearskin rug. It felt soft and welcoming under my feet.

I was in a dining nook that overlooked a modern kitchen full of chrome appliances. That was the only modern touch to the otherwise rustic decor. The entire house was like something out of a Swedish ski resort I could never afford. Pine wood frames looked over the lush, green mountains and the countertops were glistening with fresh polish. It was like a mountaineer's wet dream. I felt as out of place here as a dirty sneaker in a ballroom.

Two guys perched on high stools in front of the kitchen island. I recognized Zan's younger twin brothers, even though I hadn't seen them in years. They both had short-cropped hair and matching grins on their faces. One had a bowl of grapes on his lap and was throwing it toward his twin who was trying to catch them in his mouth like a dog. Both erupted into laughter when a grape hit the floor.

The one snapping at the grapes threw his arms up in the air at the sight of me.

"Green!" he exclaimed. "Christ on toast! You're looking... well, *green.*"

I couldn't help a smile. "Gee, thanks Rad."

His twin rolled his eyes. "Ignore him." One long leg pushed a chair toward me. "Sit your ass down before you fall on it."

Zandro Hrom stood behind the counter, his back to me. Hands busy flipping eggs on a sizzling hot pan, he didn't seem to hear me approach. His white tank top stretched over his muscular back and revealed a series of tattoos. Kelpies, wolves, minotaurs and demon faces glared from his skin with all the ferocity the skilled tattoo artist was capable of. And it was a lot. They looked so lifelike that after staring at them, they seemed to move. His hair was freshly washed and small droplets of water cascaded from his short pony tail. I tried not to watch as they dripped down his muscular neck. Last night had joggled some things inside me that I wasn't comfortable with. Resentment, I recognized. I'd felt it for years. But the desire wasn't a welcome newcomer. I already knew what happened when I fell for Zandro Hrom. I cleared my throat.

"Hey, Zan," I said. "Thanks... for yesterday."

Rad pumped his fist into the air. "Woot-woot!" Jaro kicked his shin.

I felt myself flush. Did Zan tell them about the kiss? No, he couldn't have, I thought. They were just being boys.

Zan cocked an eyebrow in Rad's direction. The young man grinned. Unlike me, Zan looked like he'd been relaxing at his fancy ranch for a week. A towel was thrown over his shoulder. The familiar smell of smoke and rain cut through the smell of grease and frying protein.

Turning around, he held two plates in his hands. He placed one down in front of me.

"You're welcome."

He was acting as if my sitting in his kitchen with his brothers was the most natural thing in the world. I felt myself warm, realizing that the T-shirt I wore was probably his. It remembered his body, his muscled shoulders and the flat planes of his stomach. I couldn't help but compare him to Lafayette. The incubus' beauty *slithered* like a snake in the sand. Zan's felt solid, like polished oakwood warmed by the sun.

The plate in front of me was heaped with eggs and bacon. A buttered brown toast that smelled like sourdough accompanied it.

"Rye bread," Zan said. "The real stuff. Bava bakes it from scratch."

"Bava?" Did Zan have a girlfriend? Did I care?

"Our kikimora," he said. "She and her husband are the domovois that followed us from Vyraj. They keep me and the brothers alive." He nodded a scruffy chin in Rad and Jaro's direction. They were now fighting over the second plate he'd brought. "It's a full-time job."

I smiled and poked my fork at the unreal stack of steaming eggs in front of me. It was like Zan was trying to feed a werewolf. I wasn't particularly hungry, but I took a glass of orange juice.

"So." He leaned over the kitchen island as I chewed. Grey eyes narrowed. "What were you doing in Demon Bazaar, Chrys?"

I almost choked on my juice, but I wasn't about to stop drinking this freshly squeezed goodness. Citrus burst on my tongue. This was no bottled crap.

"I don't know, Zan," I said. "What were you doing stalking me?"

His cheek twitched. "Aren't you and the reaper supposed to be suspended? What were you doing slinking around the Bazaar?"

I picked up a slice of crispy bacon.

"Shopping."

He cocked an eyebrow.

Crossing his arms over his chest, he did his best to stare me down. "Rad saw you go into Circus Circus," he said. "I did the math."

"I was gambling with grandmas!" the twin said with a grin.

"By the time I got there," Zan continued. "You were already marching right into a trap in Inc and Suc."

"Oh, and would you leave your partner behind to be enslaved?" I asked casually.

"I'm—"

I pouted and batted my eyes. "A big strong demigod? And I'm just a poor, weak dragon spawn?"

"*Not* on an incubus' hit list," Zan finished. His hands tightened into fists over his biceps, and it seemed to take some effort for him not to punch the table. "You should've let me kill him."

There it was again, the murder in his eyes. I didn't let myself think about what it meant.

"How very humanitarian of you," I said.

We glowered at each other, and I refused to look away. With a towel over his shoulder, he looked less like a thunder demigod and more like a host of a Tattooed Chef reality TV show.

"He touched you without permission. I should've opened his belly," Zan said.

Whose permission, mine or yours? I wanted to ask, but that would be wandering down some dangerous roads, and I wasn't going down that road with Zan again. I knew exactly where it ended.

"He knew something," I told him. "He said that whoever is leading the demons had incubus blood."

Zan frowned. "Anything else?"

I shook my head. "It's possible that he was trying to rattle me. But I don't think so."

"I'll look into it," he said. "Maybe I need to pay your *sweetie* another visit."

His eyes flicked to my lips and I knew he was thinking about the kiss. Oh, that *kiss*. The memory of it made desire shoot through my belly.

"Don't," was all I said. We stared at each other, neither willing to be the first to bring it up.

Laughter interrupted our stand-off. Jaro and Rad had wolfed down what was left of the breakfast and were now taking turns showing off their flexes and measuring the widths of their biceps against one another.

Zan shook his head. "I hope that's the only thing they measure."

I suppressed a straight up girlish giggle. This felt too good. Sitting down to a delicious breakfast with people that felt something like family. I was an only child, and every time we made a stop at a commune to weather a winter or to take a break from the never-ending RV parks, a family setting like this was both exotic and magical. The commune Lizzy lived in had been my favorite. The commune Lizzy *died* in, I reminded myself. Soul-eating dragons don't wake up to hot breakfasts. I pushed away my plate.

"So," I said, "how goes the mighty warrior's mighty demon hunt?"

Zan's eyes turned from cloudy to stormy and I knew the answer. "We're on their track."

I narrowed my eyes at him. "Bullshit. They went underground, didn't they? You guys can't spot them in eagle form."

He pulled the towel over his shoulder and slapped it on the counter. He wiped at a non-existent grease stain so hard I thought he'd strip off the wood polish.

"Someone is guiding them, I'm sure of it," he said at last. "He knows our terrain."

I chewed on my lip. "Where could they be going?"

"Black Rock Desert," Rad piped in, taking a break from needling his brother. Zan frowned at him. "What?" He looked between the two of us. "I thought it was obvious? If the devourers want to keep riding the power train, they need to take the souls to an energy source and bust in. Burning Man happens in the Black Rock Desert every year. That's like eighty thousand people pumping their energy into the place. There is gotta be energetic reserves for miles under that dust."

Zan shook his head. "Yes, if they wanted *living* energy. Demons feed on the dead."

I agreed with Zan.

"What if they're looking for *dead* energy?" I asked Rad. "Where would they go?"

The twin shrugged.

Chewing on my lip, I considered telling Zan about Tick. I had little evidence, but maybe it wouldn't hurt for them to know that someone had found a soul husk in the middle of the desert. Maybe the knowledge would help.

"Listen, Zan—"

With a loud pop, the kikimora—Bava—materialized in the air. She was accompanied by a prune-faced little man. I almost fell off my chair, but the brothers just looked at them expectantly.

"Urgent message from the valkyrie Astrid," the man said. His creepy yellow eyes gave lemurs a run for their money. Bava's husband, the house domovoi, I guessed. "She spotted what looks like a demon trail in Fernley."

Fernley was on the way to Black Rock Desert. Rad high-fived Jaro. "Told you! Playa, here we come!"

Zan didn't look convinced, but he pointed to each brother. "Rad, get our weapons. Jaro, locate Astrid."

I pulled my phone out of my pocket. "Signal?"

They shook their heads.

"We're too high up," Jaro said. "You might get some luck around the property, but I wouldn't count on it."

Of course. They got up in eagle form and had magical messengers, so who cares about a little thing like modern tech?

"Take me with you," I said to Zan. "I can help."

"You're supposed to be suspended," he said. "Keep your nose out of this, Chrys."

"Why?" I demanded. "Because I'm Veles' daughter and you want to keep me away from souls?" I stabbed my finger on the table. "Get in line."

"If I wanted to keep you away from souls, I'd let you run around playing detective and get *killed*," he said. "Or worse." A slow, wicked smile stretched Zan's mouth and I realized why he had taken me up here and not, say, the

ERS headquarters. "Luckily, you're my *honored guest* now." He turned to Bava and added in Old Slav. "Make sure she's well taken care of."

The kikimora bowed. "Yes, master."

"You basta—" I started, but the brothers already weren't listening to me. Springing to their feet, they moved like the well-oiled machine they were. Rad and Jaro pulled their jackets out of the closet. Jaro tossed Zan his leather jacket and he caught it in mid-air. The familiar scent of rain and feathers hit my senses. Two minutes ago, I was ready to tell Zan about Tick. Now anger simmered inside me. "Zan. You can't just trap me in your luxury home. I can be an asset to your search."

He ignored me.

"I'll see you on the launch pad," Zan told Jaro, who nodded and sprinted toward his respective task. He winked at me. "Enjoy Perun's hospitality."

"I thought the only hospitality Perun has for me is an axe in the gut," I said to Zan. No one said I was above being petty when pissed.

The corners of his mouth fell into a frown. "Listen, Chrys—"

"Five minutes!" Rad shouted from the doorway.

Zan turned back to me. "Stay put," he stabbed at my chest with his finger. "For your own good."

Without another word, he pushed open the screen door that led onto the balcony and the breathtaking view of the mountains outside. The eagle burst into the air with a predatory screech, off to hunt prey he was born to hunt. I watched him disappear into the air and finished my orange juice. A certain smug calmness replaced my anger. It seemed that Zan wasn't paying attention in the years that he'd known me. "Staying put" wasn't in my repertoire.

14

M<small>Y RESOLVE BEGAN TO</small> budge when I realized that Zan was smarter than I'd given him credit for. At first glance, "staying put" seemed like the most viable option. There were very few places for me to go here that wouldn't cause broken legs. Not to mention the domovois. The house spirits were fiercely loyal, and fiercely nosey. I'm sure they saw spying on their master's "guest"—who also happened to be an American by-blow of his fiercest enemy—as their solemn duty. When I went upstairs to take stock of the items I had access to, I could feel their owlish eyes following me from the shadows. Domovois could appear and disappear at will. The house they protected and served was their territory, and there wasn't a space they weren't privy to. After walking through every room in the house, looking for a signal, I was desperately wishing that my shifter form had wings, too.

In my room, I took stock of my possessions. The hooded denim jacket and my shredded tank top I wore to the Bazaar had been washed. My boots looked polished and smelled like Febreze. Now that was just straight-up judgy of the domovois. My wallet and the ERS key fob survived yesterday's fall, as did my badge. Tick's seal was intact, too, and my eyes lingered on it. Zan didn't want my help. That was fine. It didn't mean that I was going to sit on my ass and let more soul husks drop on the sand of Nevada. I needed to find the smuggler, but first I needed to bust out of this stupid, gorgeous ranch. Everything fit neatly into the pockets of my jeans and jacket. I'm not a purse kind of girl. I had fired a few salt rounds at Inc and Suc, but the gun was still mostly loaded. I also still had two full salt cartridges, and one of silver filings. I put them, and the gun, into the holsters on my belt and closed my jacket over them. Then I tucked Zan's shirt into my jeans.

Heading down the stairs, I managed not to jump when Bava popped up in front of me.

"Where are you going, honored guest?" Her spookily pleasant smile could fry a roach in its tracks. "Master bid Bava to give our guest her full attention."

Trying to look casual, I pulled the phone out of my pocket. I waved it.

"Need to call my superiors," I said. "Going to walk around the property."

Her yellow eyes widened. "Master Zan wouldn't like that very much. Best you stay put." The eerily pleasant smile stretched all the way to her ears and showed a row of narrow, pointy teeth.

A part of me wanted to tell her where "master Zan" could shove his opinions. I thought better of it. Somehow, I knew that if she put her mind to it, she could make me stay. Her magic wasn't strong, but it was very specific, and she was the real mistress of the house. She could probably get me lost in the endless maze of Eagle Nest's rooms. Slavic spirits were good at that. I had to play it smart.

I put a hand on my hip. "Is Jaro not your master, too?"

Her eyes widened. "Of course master Jaro is master, he is master indeed!"

"Well," I drawled. "Well, master *Jaro* said I could look for a signal around the property."

Walking past the momentarily stunned kikimora, I went to the kitchen and toward the porch beyond the sliding door.

Bava popped up in front of me. "Master Zan—"

"Probably wouldn't like it if you questioned Master Jaro's authority," I said confidently. In fact, I had no idea what the pecking order was between the brothers. I just hoped it was enough to get me out of the house.

"But—" She waved her finger. "I think Bava knows what you are doing."

I raised my eyebrows. "Do you want your Masters to argue over this small matter? I'll be right back."

Bava hesitated. "If you will be, Bava will wait," she said after a pause.

"Yep," I said brightly and slid open the screen door. The air outside was so fresh you could drink it and I breathed in a lungful of pine needles. "Be right back!"

I had no such intention, of course. I felt a little bad for the house spirit. What I said wasn't entirely a lie—I needed to get a hold of Rudy. But finding a cell signal was only a part of the agenda. What I really needed to do was find Zan's Jeep.

I couldn't guess where he'd left it. When I was a safe distance from the Nest, I circled the house in search of a path down. My best guess was that he'd parked it somewhere and carried me the rest of the way. Maybe I wouldn't even have to break into it. I doubted Zan was worried about his property this high up. Being a demon-slaying badass can make one careless. Unlocked car, and maybe keys conveniently left inside? I wouldn't put it past the arrogant son of Perun.

Half an hour later, I swore as a branch hit me in the face for a hundredth time. I could barely see the Nest if I craned my neck uphill. Another half hour passed, and I was sweaty and my head throbbed. Where had Zan parked the damned thing? My plan was getting less brilliant by the minute, and getting lost in the woods was becoming more and more likely. I sat on a stump and stretched out my legs. I really must've been concussed. Shortness of breath wasn't normal for me. My vision swam. I probably hit my head much harder than I initially thought. At the very least, I should have eaten that breakfast. That delicious orange juice sat all by itself in my stomach and had turned to nausea. I didn't have time for this. Neither did the souls whom Zan was undoubtedly *not* rescuing. The thought of returning to the Nest and waiting for the infuriating thunder god made me grind my teeth. I was a rescuer, damn it, not a damsel.

As I leaned over to tighten the laces on my boots, I heard a soft crunch come from my pocket. I frowned and slid my fingers under the denim. A soft plastic shape fit into my palm.

The ERS van key fob.

"No," I said out loud to the idea that flashed through my brain. "Stonefield would kill me."

Or fire me. Maybe literally, being a djinn and all. I was already treading the knife's edge as it was. As far as he knew, I was sipping kombucha in mom's RV like a good girl. I needed to keep looking for the truck. My phone vibrated in my pocket.

My elation of somehow finding signal was dampened by the fact that the person calling was my boss.

"Hey Chief!" I chirped into the speaker. "I was just thinking to call you."

"Green," his pleasant baritone hummed in my ear. "I've been calling all day. Why can't I get a hold of you and Mort?"

I swore under my breath. Rudy wasn't one to ignore chief's calls, which meant he wasn't in the human world.

"Ah," I said. What was I supposed to tell him? That the reaper took a tropical vacation? "I think Rudy was doing some research on—" What did he even do in his free time? "Lake Tahoe's selkies and such. Maybe he's got no signal?"

I wanted to smack my forehead as I waited for a response. Who'd taught me to lie? George Washington?

"Fine. And where are you?" he growled.

The second lie came easier. Lean into what he expects.

"Hiking in the Sierras with my mom," I said. He mumbled something into the phone, and I decided not to push my luck. "How's the investigation?" I asked. "Did you find them?"

I already knew they hadn't, of course. Still, my heart drummed as I waited for the answer.

"No," he said. "Stonefield isn't happy."

I nodded. "I imagine not."

"We found hellhound tracks near the sinkhole," he said after a pause. "The devourers brought them along."

Gripping my phone, I felt sweat break out on my forehead. This is why I'd heard the howling.

"Did you find any soul husks?" I asked.

"I promised to keep you updated, Green, but I still don't want you involved," Chief Baran said. "And no."

No wonder the Hrom brothers couldn't spot the devourers. Hellhounds could turn themselves and their riders invisible. Also, I realized I was wrong. There were no soul husks littering the Nevada desert. The hellhounds wouldn't let one hit the ground before gobbling it up.

Each one of those souls was a person. A person who had lived a life, had hopes and dreams, a family. Some unknown trespass had landed them in Hell. And now, each one the demons drained wouldn't have another chance at life.

"I see," I said. I don't know what my voice sounded like, but I did my best to school it. Zan was right. I owed

Chief my job, and for the years that he'd looked out for me. "Thank you for letting me know."

He humphed. Static rustled in my ear. "I hope you and Rudy take some much-needed time off while we handle this. Maybe you should join him at the *lake*." I could hear a smile in his voice, and couldn't help my own. He clicked off, and I stared at the key fob between my hands. I called Rudy and wasn't surprised when it went straight to voicemail. This time, I was on my own. At least I didn't have to involve another person in my dangerous decisions.

If there was no trail of soul husks, this meant that Tick was the last to find one. I was running out of energy and time. The key fob sitting on my knee hummed with energy. I could use a surge to get off the mountain. The van's navigation could find almost anyone in Yav. Tick's location could be mine with just a click of a button.

I pointed the fob at a small clearing between the pine trees in front of me. Nothing happened for several long minutes. Maybe I had been wrong to think that the van would just find me. Maybe, Uncle Ophis had wired it to only work in Reno. Maybe my suspension had revoked my magical rights to summon it to my aid.

The ground trembled. Leaves and pine needles shook off trees. I rose to my feet, a familiar thrill rumbling in my chest. This was exactly what I loved the most—my rescue van coming to me in the time of need. The ground crumbled, clumps of earth parting as the van emerged from the moss like some sort of predatory ant. The roof was smeared with mud and the window wipes slid across the glass to clear the dirt and debris.

"Hello, beautiful," I murmured. Zan could keep his manly Jeep. My rescue van could drive circles around it. I pulled on the door and slid into the sweet-smelling salon. "Good seeing you."

The seals and the wards flashed blue and purple as the magic flowed through the upholstery and the enchanted metal. Uncle Ophis had done a stellar job on maintenance this month. That wasn't surprising. The man was a genius. I'd always been jealous of his talent for taking a thing and connecting it to the universe as seamlessly as grafting a branch onto an apple tree. The van sparked with fresh energy, all damage from our escape from the devourers gone. I felt grimy as I put my foot on the gas pedal. The controls over my head pulsed and flashed with familiar efficiency. I pulled down the GPS panel and smoothed Tick's summoning circle out on my lap. I couldn't summon the demon spawn, but I could track them down. From the symbols I could glean on the page, the spiritual signature of the demon was starting to take shape. Tick the smuggler was a quarter demon, a shifter of some kind. They didn't quite belong in Yav, their home was supposed to be Hell. I mean, I wasn't the one to judge a supernatural by-blow that preferred the comforts—and easy scores—of living on Earth. Yet, they were never caught. Or didn't stay caught. The Demon Bazaar wasn't their home, either. This meant that they were good at hiding, someone who could blend into the shadows. A trickster. Probably using their shifter nature to stay low.

I turned on the keypad and typed in:

Tick the Smuggler, Spawn of demonkin, Trickster archetype 1.

The contents of the screen disappeared, and an hourglass replaced it. It turned over and over in my vision. I tapped my fingers on the dashboard and waited. It was taking long enough to make a frown crease my aching forehead. Were they really that good at hiding that an ERS van designed to track down anything and anyone in the Underworlds couldn't find a simple demon spawn in Yav?

A map replaced the hourglass. My eyes burrowed into the red dot sitting on a curving line that marked a river. Frown deepening, I rubbed my temple on the off chance my eyes were actually deceiving me. I had expected a ping in Seattle. Or at least, in Vegas, where the smugglers loved to pawn off the shadier wares onto the dragons that guarded the vaults of the casinos. But no, the dot was much closer than that.

"Truckee River, Downtown Reno," I read out loud. "You've got to be kidding me."

Tick, the evasive smuggler that even Step couldn't track down without a seal, was literally in my backyard.

15

It would be a waste of the inter-pantheon surge to teleport straight there. Turning on the all-terrain mode, I navigated my way down the mountain. The funny thing was that I did find the road down that Zan must've used to drive up his Jeep. A mischievous part of my heart wanted to go up there and steal it anyway. Out of spite. It had nothing to do with sitting in the car surrounded by his scent, of course.

The heat was baking the road into puddles of mirage by the time I got to the city. The River Trail of the Truckee River curves around the inner sanctum of Downtown. Pots of flowers and charming benches mark its length. This was a great place for a date. That's what people tell me, anyway. Maybe Tick was enjoying a beer at one of the restaurants that lined the water. Parking the truck along the street, I followed the trail to where the red blinking dot had pointed me.

A splash and a scream echoed from the riverbank. It didn't seem to attract the attention of an old lady who was walking her poodle along the trail. That was all kinds of weird. I bolted to the source of the noise and drew out my gun as I ran. Before I could judge the old lady for her callousness, I saw a ripple of an illusion shrouding the shallow water of where the water thinned over shallow rock. Three freakishly big horses were stomping around. Water splashed up their green hides. Kelpies. What were they doing this far from their lakes? Shouting and neighing erupted, and I quickened my pace.

A person of medium height and orange hair was the source of the commotion. They fell back and forth, trying to defend themselves. I didn't see a weapon, but a shimmer in the air seemed to help them along. It was too far to see. What I *did* see was the bright red blood running down their face and disappearing into the collar of their poncho.

Tick wasn't enjoying a beer. They were getting the shit kicked out of them.

The kelpies herded their prey away from the shore. I looked past the green-black hides and saw that the water elementals weren't trying to kill the demon spawn outright. They were doing what they loved most—drowning the culprit in deeper water. Another monster would've been satisfied with just hoofing their prey to death. But kelpies harvest soul power from the waters. Once you were pushed into the depths, you didn't come out.

Tick and I realized that at the same time. The red-haired trickster was cornered, and I didn't blame them when the color drained from their face. What had they done to piss the water demons off to this staggering degree? The Reno kelpies knew all too well what happened to those who broke the Spiral's laws and drowned anyone who even passed for a human. The reminder was pumping water in the walkway between Circus Circus and Silver Legacy. My eyes drifted past the panicked trickster and the water horses set on their demise. They landed on an object reflecting the sunlight. It was a dark green egg, covered with slime and weeds. It looked like it'd been dragged out from the bottom of the river. I swore and reached for the cartridge of silver shavings on my belt. No wonder the illusion magic covered the area. Illusion magic is a natural defense mechanism for supernatural monsters. Especially the young. Kelpies don't live in the Truckee river, preferring the depths of the nearby lakes like Tahoe and Pyramid Lake. Better to drown people with. Shallow water is where they lay their eggs, and that was a kelpie egg. My invaluable source of information wasn't getting out alive if I didn't act immediately.

Quickly swapping the half-empty salt cartridge with one loaded with silver, I aimed at the nearest kelpie. Maybe I could distract it enough to give the demon time to escape. The gun shot filled my ears, and I saw the brief shine of the shavings as they dotted the air before dotting the hide of the monstrous horse. The kelpie bucked, its hooves rearing back and its eyes rolling in its head. I jumped into the water, no longer trying for the element of surprise. My boots broke through water and hit the soft mud beneath. I whirled on to the second horse and shot its haunches full of silver shavings, too. It wouldn't kill them, but it would take a couple of days for their skin to turn over enough to evacuate the silver poison. Really, the kelpies weren't wrong to be pissed. This is what happened when you messed with their babies. It should've been Tick who got a hide full of salt. The kelpies' red eyes turned all of their fury on me, and I forgot all about feeling self-righteous. I lunged to the side as the first kelpie barreled into me. My elbows split the water and I could feel my skin split as it met the rocks beneath.

I just rolled out of the way of oncoming hooves when the second kelpie caught up to the first and smashed its legs down. Their manes whipped back and forth as they stamped down on around me like I was a well-lit cockroach. I moved purely on instinct as I rolled under their bellies. Water went into my mouth and nose and I couldn't see much through the froth. The sound of their hooves pounding through the silt, coupled with their unnatural neighs, was deafening. I tried to yelp through the water in my mouth as a hoof struck the back of my thigh. Animal panic filled me as my head went under. I couldn't resurface. My brain screamed for oxygen. They were going to trample me to death. I pushed off with all my strength and grabbed a mouth full of oxygen before being pulled back under again. I'd definitely underestimated the effect of shooting an already pissed-off kelpie with silver. Zan did always say that rescuing every Jack and Jill would get me killed. It seemed today he would be right.

I was choking on river water when I saw an opening. I launched my body towards it. The back of my thigh, now blooming with a hoof-shaped bruise, screamed in protest. It slowed me down just enough for my opening to close. Another hoof slammed into my back. Or it would've, if I'd been there. Hauling myself out of the water, I stumbled over rocks before coming face to face with Tick.

"My *hero*," they said.

I hyperventilated through watery coughs while Tick's grinning face loomed over me. Had they just stood there while I was being pummeled to death on their behalf? Charming.

I didn't have time to reply as the kelpie's stomping frenzy stopped. They might've gotten curious about why they weren't hitting soft flesh anymore. They wheeled and spotted us, and I scrambled to my feet. The universe's attempt to give me a clean shirt that wasn't covered in blood had been short-lived.

I grabbed Tick's elbow, and we ran down the shoreline like death was chasing us. Which it was. As we sloshed our way past the shore where the glistening egg had been sitting, Tick's eyes filled with avarice. They twisted out of my grasp and, with a wink, blurred in my vision. I saw their mage hand ripple through the air, sparkling. The kelpies were now focused solely on me, and the trickster decided to use this opportunity to grab their prize. Not on my watch.

"Oh no, you don't!" I swapped the silver with the half-empty salt cartridge in my gun as I ran, and hoped water hadn't gotten into it. Feeling like James Bond, I aimed dramatically at the sparkling shape. Luckily, my dragon knew exactly where the shifter was. Their soul was a tangible thing to me, even if their body was invisible. I fired a round of salt in Tick's direction and heard a yelp as the trickster stumbled sideways into the water. Their camouflage spell had dispelled as their concentration fell apart. I had to get us both up onto the walkway that circled the river, because kelpies couldn't follow us very far out of the water. Not slowing my pace, I grabbed Tick by the poncho and hauled them to their feet.

"Go! Go!" I said as I pointed up the bank. They seemed to come to their senses, putting one foot in front of the other. I followed them in their flight, hopping up and over the railing of the walkway. We both landed badly, slamming onto the boards of the bridge, and lay there panting on blessedly dry land.

The kelpies paced beneath us. Water splashed as they stomped their anger and nipped at each other in bloody fury. I poked my head down, knowing that they wouldn't be able to come after me now. Reno was the Spiral's territory, and they had no proper cause to harm me. Not that they agreed. I wasn't sure I would either if I had an ass full of silver like they did.

"No harm done," I said. "Right, guys?"

They bared their crooked yellow teeth up at me. Okay, then.

A sound of slapping bare feet came from behind me. I didn't think. Whipping around on my knees, I pointed my gun at Tick's back. I wasn't even sure there was another round of salt left.

"Going somewhere?" I asked.

Tick stopped mid-flight and slowly turned around. The bruising on their face did nothing to lessen the brightness of their grin. Bright orange hair was sticking to their forehead in playful curls. I could see black roots peeking from under the bright color. I inspected them. Their horns were smaller than mine and thrust out of their forehead. A guardian demon, I guessed. They patrolled the highest levels of Hell, and so it was pretty common for them to sneak up into Yav, stealing and breeding with humans. Tick's eyes were a shiny beetle-brown.

Their shoulders lifted in a casual shrug, as if being held at gunpoint was just another Tuesday. "It was worth a shot," they said.

"Was the egg worth a shot, too?" I asked. "You could've died."

"Live fast, die young," they said. Not even their bravado could hide how hard they were breathing. "I'm not complaining, but who are you?"

It took me a couple of tries, but I pulled out my badge. The golden ammonite glinted in the sun. I could feel blood congealing under multiple bruises that bloomed on my body. I had stretched my demigod resilience too thin these last few days.

"ERS," I said, watching the corners of their smile droop with utmost satisfaction. "You're coming with me."

I kept my arm firm around Tick's shoulder as I marched them to the car. I couldn't just walk them down the street while pointing a gun at them. That was the surest way to get the human police to call the authorities and complicate things. Frankly, I was sure that Tick had enough illusion magic to camouflage us both. But, of course, they wouldn't bother.

We made it to the truck without incident, and I shoved them through the barn door. The wards inside hummed, sensing a soul. They weren't going anywhere now. Just to be sure, I handcuffed them. The shimmering hand slithered from under Tick's poncho and waved at me.

"Don't even think about it," I murmured. Tick looked amused by the entire operation. That made me nervous. After the performance with the kelpies, they were being a bit too cooperative.

"What are my charges exactly, Doll Face?" Tick asked, voice syrupy. "I'm feeling a bit triggered here."

Both of us looked triggered. We were soaking wet, bleeding, and out of breath. That didn't matter. I had a job to do. I made myself move past the pain and straightened in my soaking-wet jacket like I had some authority here. Stolen van and all.

"One count of theft of magical and tribal property, and a count of trespass." I gave Tick a firm shake of my head. "It doesn't look good."

Tick's eyes narrowed. "Don't talk to me about tribal property, *wasichu*." So much for Doll Face. I've traveled through various communities all over the country. I recognized a slur when I heard it, especially a Native American one.

"Paiute?" I asked, guessing at a tribe native to Nevada.

"Lakota."

"You're a demon spawn," I cocked my head. "And Native American?"

"Oh, gee! How did you guess?" Tick said. "They way I see it, you just wrongfully arrested me on the basis of discrimination. I have rights."

I would not let them rattle me. Eyes narrowing, I leaned against the open door of the truck.

"I don't suppose saving your *life* is going to cut me some slack?" I asked.

Tick scoffed, their expression becoming smug. "Judging by the fact that you're without your partner, and looking over your shoulder like you're the one stealing kelpie eggs, you're not exactly authorized to hold me."

I tapped my lip as if thinking about it.

"You have me there, sport. I do wonder, though... What will happen if I turn you in for trying to pawn a soul husk at the Demon Bazaar?"

Tick paled. I had finally hit a nerve.

"I don't have it anymore," they said faintly. At least they had the decency to sound repulsed. Good. Touching soul husks is bad luck, a major loss of karmic points. There is a reason Step had looked like I'd accused him of trafficking dead bodies.

I raised my eyebrows. "So, you admit it."

"Look, lady," Tick said. They sounded a lot less sure of themselves now. "I'm just passing through. This side of Nevada isn't even my territory. I got off the beaten path."

Their eyes widened like a puppy who had peed on the rug. "Lost my way?"

I fought hard not to roll my eyes. The trickster gave me another wide smile. The shimmering mage hand over their head gave me a peace sign.

Standing in my soaking wet clothes was making me shiver. I was aching and probably bleeding again. I didn't want to do this. Gods knew the last thing I wanted to do was take a stranger to my messy sanctum sanctorum. But it wasn't like I could take them to the Spiral interrogation room.

"Come on," I said. "Let's go somewhere more comfortable and discuss our options."

They perked up. "Can I ride shotgun?"

"Absolutely not."

I swung the van doors in their face.

My socks slurping in my boots, I walked around and slid into the driver seat. My vision doubled. At least I could see my apartment building from here.

Time to give Mittens the shock of his life. I had a guest.

16

I PARKED THE VAN in the building parking lot and surveyed the late afternoon space. It looked like the residents of the Tower were still at their soul-killing day jobs. I rubbed the spot between my eyes where a headache thrummed.

"Hey, lady," Tick's voice rose from the back. "I'm starting to feel neglected back here. Are you taking me to the slammer or what?"

Turning off the engine, I flipped on the camouflage mode and marched to the back of the van. The seals sparked as I pulled the barn doors open. Tick was sitting cross-legged on the stretcher. The ghostly mage hand waved at me from their shoulder. One of the lollipops we kept for diabetic rescues stuck out between their teeth. I wondered what else the poncho hid. *Damn*, I was in over my head. I wasn't qualified to contain miscreants. Or babysitting. I was a "fetch and deliver" kind of girl.

My brows drew together in a way I hoped made me look fierce and not a like a migraine-ridden old clerk.

"A detour," I said and slapped the gun at my hip. "I'm nice and fast with this thing, so don't try anything funny."

With an exaggerated sigh, Tick waved their handcuffed wrists toward me. "Yes, daddy."

Upstairs, I paused in front of my door. Tick snickered as I fumbled with my keys.

"Want me to pop that open for you?" they asked.

I lowered the ward at my front door briefly to allow Tick inside. The familiar scents of my apartment—the lingering smell of Thai takeout and the incense—made a knot loosen in my chest. This was my space, saturated with my demi influence. I could re-group here.

"Wow," Tick said as they looked over my bare walls and tatty furniture. "I didn't know straight girls lived like frat boys in Reno. What's happened to the hetero-normative agenda?" They switched to a stage whisper. "Are you secretly a psycho?"

I glared at them. "Sit." I pointed at my couch, then hesitated. We were both still soaking wet, and only the April warmth was keeping us from shaking in our skivvies. "Hang on. Take off your poncho. I'll dry it."

Tick's eyebrows flew up into their shaggy hairline. "A sicko, then!" When I responded with a "suit yourself" look, they shifted their shoulders. The first look of discomfort crossed their features. "Yeah, okay."

I freed one of their wrists and we did an awkward dance as Tick shrugged off the poncho. Underneath, they wore a white tank top that stretched over narrow shoulders and a wiry frame. They sniffed as I pushed them toward the couch.

"Anything here I should be concerned about?" I asked. "Magic threads? Pockets of another dimension? Gentle cycle?"

Tick grinned up at me. "This is the nicest kidnapping I've ever had. We're not picky. Medium heat is fine."

I resisted the perverted desire to sniff the poncho. Magic pulsed from it, as if the threads under my fingers were alive. Maybe they were. The demon spawn was a sort of demi, after all.

Tick kicked off their shoes and put their feet on my coffee table. I wrinkled my nose at their soggy, mismatched socks. I had found my coffee table at a garage sale ten years ago, but still. I pushed their feet off with the heel on my boot.

"Stay here."

Tick raised the handcuffs. "You're the boss."

I didn't dare to waste time on a shower. Doing my best with my hair, I pulled it back into a ponytail and surveyed the damage where my horn used to be. The purple was turning into a sickly orange, but it no longer throbbed. I changed into a fresh tank top and a fresh pair of jeans. Moving quickly, I tossed my jacket in with Tick's poncho. Water-logged denim got pushed into the corner and Zan's shirt got folded on the counter. I didn't have domovois doing my laundry. The dryer hummed as it beat the clothes around. Sitting on a closed toilet, I took a deep breath. I'd managed to find the trickster, and the rest I could play by ear. I could do this. Picking up my Docs, I shouldered the bathroom door. The sunlight on the balcony would make quick work of drying them.

Something struck me across the face. A resounding slap deafened me. The back of my head met the wall behind me as a hand gripped my windpipe. Dropping from my hand, my Docs clattered onto the ground. I raked at the claw gripping me and found nothing but air. In fact, all I saw was air. Glittering, shimmering air that was transparent enough to see a face.

Tick wasn't grinning anymore. They were sitting on my kitchen stool, their elbows resting on their bony knees as they surveyed me. Fingers steepled over handcuff-less wrists.

"I think we should chat," Tick said. "Don't you?"

I struggled against the wall, suspended in mid-air. My heels kicked against it. I grabbed for the gun at my belt.

"Uh-uh-uh," Tick said. A dazzling flash and the gun was in their hand. Red hair swung over their forehead as the trickster inspected the cartridge loaded into it.

"Ocean salt," they said and sniffed. "Enchanted for demon paralysis. Spiral-grade." They slid the cartridge back and smiled at the satisfying click. "Fancy. Should fetch a good price on the black market."

I clawed at the spirit hand as I felt blood going to my cheeks. Panic filled my brain as the oxygen left it.

The trickster squinted up at me, their eyes two slits of menace. "Who hired you? Was it the Angels? The Russians? The dragons?"

Tick wasn't trying to kill me. At least, I didn't think so. That didn't mean that being attacked on own turf didn't piss me the hell off.

My dragon surged in my chest and filled my ears with a roar. The crystal on my wrist thrashed on its chord. I didn't like when she took control, but the quickly departing oxygen in my brain told me I didn't have much choice.

Small goat, little goat, come to my stead. Old Slav words surfaced in my mind of their own accord. It pulled toward Tick. *Come to me, stay with me, not there but here instead.*

The scales surged up my arms and I felt the familiar golden pulse come from my chest. My chest turned into a magnet as it reached across the kitchen and to Tick's core.

The demon spawn's eyes widened. They gasped and dropped my gun. I wasn't familiar with the sensation of something yanking on my soul within my body, but from what I'd heard, it wasn't pleasant. Like "someone grabbing a handful of your innards and pulling" was how Rudy had phrased it. I couldn't pull a living soul out of a body, but Tick didn't know that. They paled and clawed at their chest. The shimmering air around my throat disappeared, and I plummeted to the ground. Thanks to the hours of running the obstacle course with ERS demon hunters, I didn't embarrass myself by falling on my ass.

Tick, however, did fall off the stool. Their body jerked, and I gave it another good long moment before I wrestled down my dragon. I picked up my gun and pointed the barrel between their eyes.

"What is *wrong* with you?" I said. "Really?"

Tick shrugged. "I don't know. I'm just here for the ride. Curiosity." They grinned. "Violence."

Their mage hand back handed me. I stumbled back, and the gun went off. Salt pellets shot holes in the ceiling. There went my security deposit. Tick scrambled away, and I scrambled after them. A loud knock on the door made us both freeze. Who the hell could that be?

Tick sprung up to their feet, and into a defensive stance, teeth bared. They looked like a red-haired raccoon ready to mess me up. I paused with my gun in the air. This was becoming increasingly ridiculous.

"Okay," I panted. "Okay. Let's all just take a deep breath."

Raising the gun in one hand, I pointed it at the ceiling.

"You're right," I said finally. "I'm technically suspended and poking my nose where it doesn't belong." The knocking became increasingly impatient. "That could be my boss." I pointed over my shoulder. "If I don't answer, he might shoot through the lock. I don't think either of us wants that."

Tick gave me a long, suspicious look. After a long moment, the mage hand waved at me to proceed.

"Okay," they said. "Go get it."

I wasn't sure they wouldn't ambush me, but I didn't have a choice. Praying to all the gods of the Underworlds, I slid my gun into its holster. Please don't let it actually be Chief Baran. Or worse, *Stonefield.*

Excuses forming on my lips, I pulled the door open. Words froze as I looked down on a little white-haired lady wearing bunny slippers. Her eyes blinked up at me with near-sighted bleariness. Mittens was a ghostly shape in her arms. His whiskers twitched, and his eyes burrowed into mine in mild accusation. Like, where have you been?

"Mrs. Lehmann?"

"I don't know how he keeps getting out!" she said. "You keep that door locked tighter than my dead husband's liquor cabinet!" She patted Mittens on the head. "What a sneaky boy, yes, you are."

Pleased with the attention, Mittens meowed. I looked down at my elderly neighbor in mild shock. Her sudden, adorable appearance clashed with the last two days of my life. Some humans could see ghosts, and Mrs. Lehmann was one of them. I didn't know if she'd developed the ability in old age, or had simply forgotten about having it. Either way, Mittens enjoyed the attention, which was probably why he kept crossing the walls between our apartments to grace Mrs. Lehmann with his kingly presence. He looked smug as my neighbor rubbed under his chin. Dead or alive, cats are cats.

Feeling like a character in a sitcom, I reached out my hands to take him

"I must've left my door open this morning," I said slowly. "Thank you."

"What are neighbors for?" She beamed a toothless smile. "Did you give him my little present from the other day?"

Guiltily, I remembered the paper bag rotting in the trash.

"Yep," I said.

"Oh, goodness!" her neck stretched as she glimpsed Tick over my shoulder. Her face creased with delight. "You have a guest?" she asked.

"Yes," I said, since there was nothing else to say. "I do... have a guest."

She clapped her tiny hands together. "Darling, I thought I would never see the day. Good for you." Muttering a song in German, she shuffled back down the hall.

My arms full of cat, I turned back into my apartment.

Tick was still looking at me like they were a raccoon. Except, this time, it's seen an apple in the trash. Their arms shot out.

"Kitty!"

Tick was back on my couch with Mittens on their lap. They looked perfectly content as they stroked the ghostly fur. Mittens purred, oblivious. Traitor.

I didn't bother with the handcuffs this time. Obviously, they were useless. I sat across on the armchair, blocking the window. My gun sat on my armrest in clear view, but not a threat. Yet.

"There's no point in running, you know," I said. I pulled the damp sheet of lined paper from my back pocket and unfolded the seal.

Tick's arms tightened around the cat. "Where'd you get that?" they asked.

I could see the twitch in their cheek and was satisfied knowing that Stepan hadn't cheated me. I shrugged as if I hadn't blown my entire cache of favors with the vodyanoi to get it.

"I might not be authorized to hold you for anything, but your debt is mine now," I said. Their eyes were already scheming, so I added, "don't think about stealing it. I already texted it to my partner to use in case something happens to me." That's wasn't true, but they didn't need to know that.

"Okay," Tick sat back. "Fine. What do you want? Really?"

I breathed out a sigh of what I hoped didn't sound too much like relief. We were finally bargaining, which was good. I was running out of places for bruises.

"Something very simple." I rubbed my sore knuckles. "I need you to help me track the demons that left your soul husk behind."

Tick paled and whatever cockiness they still carried deflated inside of them like a balloon.

"Wha-what?"

"You know where they went, and I want to find them," I said. "That's the price of me giving the seal back to you."

They shook their head, orange ringlets flying. "Nope. No way, man."

That made me cock my head. "Why not?"

Tick looked at me like I'd lost a marble. "They're *devourers*, and they're riding *hellhounds*. You should stay the shit away from them, too."

"And why did you follow them, if they're so dangerous?"

The trickster chewed on their lip. "I need money. Lots of it," they said. "I thought a soul husk would go for some fat cabbage."

"Let me guess," I said and batted my eyes. "Your grandma is very sick and you need money for the operation?"

"Something like that," they ground through their teeth.

"Aha." I was willing to bet the sneaky demon spawn had broken into the wrong vault. No wonder they were foaming about "Angels" and "Russians and "dragons." "Is that why you tried to steal a kelpie egg?"

They shrugged. "Maybe."

"Well, unless you want to be summoned at every hour of every day," I said pointedly, "I recommend you show me where they went. The sooner I find them, the sooner you can be on your way."

Mittens meowed and stretched on Tick's lap. Little translucent nails dug into their pants. Ghostly or not, those suckers *hurt*. The demon winced. I could see that they were considering their options and not liking a single one.

"Just help me track them, okay? You've found them once." I leaned forward. "I know they're scary. I've fought them firsthand. Twice."

That got their attention.

"Are you for real?" they asked. "And you're in one piece?"

I nodded. "Hand on my heart. You've seen me with selkies." It was a stretch to praise myself like I was some mighty warrior, but the truth *was* that I am good in a scrap. "If we get ambushed, I'll distract them while you get away."

Tick sniffed. Their hands scratched Mittens behind the ears.

"And I will get my seal back?"

"You will," I confirmed. "Messages deleted, debt repaid."

They leaned back into the cushions.

"What was that thing that you did?" they asked. "It felt like you were... I dunno." They looked uncomfortable. "Were yanking out my lungs or my breath or something."

"That was my dragon," I said. "She can— Well." I wasn't sure telling the trickster that I was a monster wouldn't send them bursting out the door, seal or no seal. Taking a deep breath, I decided on honesty. I was too sore, too stressed, and too hungry to lie about this. "My dragon can eat human souls."

I expected revulsion or a sudden attempt to gut me and take my hide to the nearest pawnshop. The last thing I expected was a grin.

"Cool!" they said. "Maybe I'll stick around."

Confused, I blinked down at Mittens who looked as if Tick's reaction was their doing.

"I should take you on every negotiation," I told him.

17

THIS TIME, AGAINST MY better judgement, I allowed Tick to ride shotgun. The trickster sat with their legs folded and munched on a steak burrito with the bliss of a true carnivore. Eating Mexican drive-through in a stolen van with a magical smuggler told me that my life had finally lost all connection to reality. Just two days ago, I was slogging through my days with decided familiarity. Now, the only thing that hasn't happened was flying pigs. The smell of fries and grilled meat wafted around us. It filled me with a bit of hysterical glee. Probably not a good sign. I chased the food down with a Red Bull. Lunch of champions.

Tick licked the sticky hot sauce off their fingers and their mage hand dabbed their face with a napkin. It tended to them like a little ghostly butler. I chewed on my guacamole cheese fries, enjoying as the savory oil spread on my tongue. After a thought, I emptied two packs of hot sauce on top. Much better.

Finally, my curiosity got the better of me. I pointed to the shimmering hand. "Is that a summoned entity?"

Tick chewed for a couple of contemplative minutes. "Handy? Nah, he's an extension of my spirit," they said finally. "My wanagi."

I humphed. Now it made sense why the hand had dissolved when I tugged on Tick's soul.

"How did you learn about your abilities?" I asked. "Did your parents teach you to channel them?"

They shook their head. "My foster dad found me when I was three. And anyway, your dragon kicks the shit out of my hand. It's like a whole other level." They wolfed down the last of the burrito. I wondered when was the last time they ate, and how often they bothered to. Their wiry frame pointed to a lean life. Their poncho, now that it was folded on their lap, smelled faintly of incense and weed. The smell of my childhood.

"Are you from Reno?" I asked.

They shrugged. "I dunno. My father is from Rosebud. It's where he found me." At my questioning look, they clarified. "The Lakota reservation in South Dakota. I lived there until I was eight."

I nodded. "And your dad?"

Their eyes shot to me. "Is this an interrogation?"

Shaking my head, I wiped the hot sauce off my fingers. "Just wondering. My mom and I were all over the place. We sold crystals and incense on the road."

A glint of surprise crossed Tick's face. "Oh, yeah? You don't look like a nomad. Kind of like a normal." They tugged a fry out of my basket. "No offense."

I couldn't help my smile. "Not enough of a normal to go to Coachella."

Tick scowled. "Fuck Coachella."

Chuckling, I thought that my mother shared the sentiment. To her and most of the vagabond population, the highly commercialized California festival was basically a swear word. This made me warm to Tick, just a tad.

"I am a normal now. I miss it, though," I admitted. "But ERS is fine. Great, in fact."

"Yeah," Tick said slowly. "Sure."

I ignored the jab and pulled out my ancient map of Reno and the surrounding areas. Spreading it out, I smoothed the edges on the elbow rest.

"Show me where you first spotted the devourers," I said.

They leaned over, still chewing.

"There," the mage hand stabbed a finger down. "That's where I began following them."

I squinted at the tiny print. "Nixon," I read. That tracked with the direction that Rad had guessed. Black Rock Desert? Really?

"What do you think about the demons going for the living energy left by Burning Man?"

Tick shook their head. "Nah. No way. Their corpse-loving asses would explode from the happy human juju in that place." They grinned. "I've put a bit into that dust myself!"

I grinned. Somehow, I didn't doubt that the trickster made the event every year. Those curls would go great with a fur coat and EDM. Not to mention that with alcohol—and illegal substances—flowing, no one would question Handy.

Leaning back in my seat, I crossed my arms over my chest. If I only I could wait for Rudy, wherever he was. I'd called Uncle Ophis to see if he could help, and got a tangled lecture about the possibilities of his location. At least I'd gotten a promise to find him—I think. I pushed my anxiety over Rudy down. Right now, I needed to get smart quick and figure out where the devourers were heading.

"Demons are looking for souls," I said. "Dead souls." I thought about what the Chief had said, about the hellhounds. "Hellhounds are carrying them toward some big score. Whatever souls they've captured, they wouldn't have wasted them if it wasn't huge."

My finger trailed up the road printed from Nixon to Black Rock Desert. If only Rudy was here and doing research at the "lake or something." Wait. The lake. Tracing left, my finger hovered over a body of water.

"What about Pyramid Lake?"

Tick shook their head, ringlets flying. "Don't want to go there this time of year."

"Why?" I asked.

"The local Paiute tribe holds the area sacred. It's spooky in the spring. Water Babies, ya know?"

I frowned. "Water Babies?"

"Yeah, it's a legend." Tick shrugged. "They're water spirits. Super dangerous when active. People drown in Pyramid Lake like crazy."

Thinking of the selkies, I blinked in confusion. "Drowning humans is illegal. The Spiral doesn't regulate them?"

Tick scoffed. "The Spiral has no right to interfere on reservation land. Plus, the Paiute don't make it a secret. Not their fault dumb white fisherman take their boats out there."

"Where did those spirits come from?"

"People say different things," they said uneasily. "The most popular story is drowned kids, I guess. Apparently, the ancient Paiute would drown malformed babies there. Hundreds of years ago."

I gaped at them. "What?"

"To keep the tribe strong," they said heavily.

"But that's—"

"Yeah," Tick said. "Anyway, whatever the truth is, the place is bad luck."

I stared at Tick. "Dead babies. Hundreds of them."

"Thousands," Tick corrected. "Who knows how many spirits are down there."

Dread pulled through me. "Maybe, that's it." I said slowly. "That's the power the demons are going after." I swallowed, tasting bile. "Thousands of innocent souls."

The drive to the lake was filled with Tick being a fidgety child. They kept poking their fingers into various controls in the van. At one point, they hit the button that released pixie dust, which knocked them out for half an hour. The most peaceful half an hour ever. While they slept, I watched their profile and wasn't surprised that the mage hand seemed as alert as ever. It covered Tick up to the shoulders with the poncho and smoothed the hair off their brow. That made me smile, albeit a bit wistfully. I wondered what it would be like to be so in touch with your nature that it was like an old friend. Not that I wasn't in touch with mine, I reminded myself. I just needed to keep it under control. The dragon was dangerous, and the dangling charm around my wrist kept me in control. Mind over matter and all that. Still, my eyes lingered on Handy as it wrapped around Tick's shoulders like a scarf. I would bet that's how the sneak had stayed alive and hidden all these years.

I used the surge button as sparingly as possible. You never know when you need to make a quick escape. The longer I stared at my headlights illuminating the road ahead, the more I doubted myself. Water Babies seemed like a crazy story. Any lake as deep as Pyramid and Tahoe has hidden shelves and unpredictable currents. There could be a number of reasons for the drownings. Not to mention, why hadn't the lake occurred to Stonefield or Chief Baran? I stepped on the pedal and kept driving. Worst-case scenario, I'd wasted an evening. If that was the case, I would return the van and try something else.

Pyramid Lake sits in the middle of a Paiute reservation. I flashed my ERS badge instead of a permit when we stopped at the ranger station. The cougar shifter deigned to take a break from a flickering screen to inspect my badge. He prodded the shiny bit of metal with suspicion. I gave him my most reassuring smile. His eyes drifted past my standard rescuer gear and to Tick's poncho and shit-eating grin. I had to admit, we did look hella suspicious.

"A new trainee," I said. "We got a call about a disturbance at the Lake."

Tick saluted him. "Hau."

The cougar sniffed. His neck was tattooed with tribal symbols that were popular with the young Native shifter population.

"What kind of disturbance?" he asked.

"The demonic kind," I said. "Possibly. We'll be in and out."

He nodded. "Make sure you are."

I looked over at Tick as we drove away. "Yeesh. Someone has a stick up his butt."

The trickster scoffed. "That's what happens when you're used to white men coming for what's yours." They threw my badge a questioning glance. "Aren't you suspended?"

"Yep," I said. I didn't want to think what would happen if the cougar called the Spiral front desk just to check my credentials. Hopefully, he was too busy watching his Netflix soaps.

My phone vibrated, and I looked down to see the Popeye picture. Humming "Popeye the Sailor Man," I answered the phone.

"Oh Zany-boo," I chirped into the phone. "Missing me already?"

"Where are you?" he growled.

By his tone, I could guess that he already knew where I *wasn't*.

"Just running some errands," I said.

"Spare me," Zan said. "I just got a call from Henry that your van is gone."

My cheeks went cold. "Does Chief Baran know?"

"Not yet," he said.

Crap, crap, crap.

"Tell me what you're doing, Chrys," he said.

That was rich. "I'm following a lead. Which is exactly what you should be doing, instead of checking up on me."

I heard his finger tap on the phone, as if he was deciding whether to yell at me.

"Care to tell me what lead?"

"I don't know," I drawled. "What did you guys find in Fernley?"

Zan's answer was a rustling silence.

"You *ditched* me in your *house*," I said, anger simmering. "With my partner missing and devourers on the loose. If you don't want to work together, I don't either. Our fathers would approve."

I hung up on him.

Next to me, Tick snapped their fingers. "You tell him, sister."

"Stuff it," I said.

Grinning wide, they mimed zipping their mouth. Last thing I needed was for Zan to go to Chief Baran. But *damn* if that thunder god didn't drive me insane.

Our headlamps pierced the twilight and lit up sage bushes. My headlights hit the rocky shore. I stopped at the edge of the water. Beyond the glistening shimmer of the shallow waves, the sunset was taking the light with it. Rouge blushed across the horizon and colored the hilltop of the lake's namesake—a rocky pyramid that sat in the middle of the mirror-like water. The surface barely carried a ripple as the darkness claimed the sky. It was peaceful. Far too peaceful.

I climbed out of the van and squinted across the surface of the lake. I wasn't sure what I was looking at. Where were the demons? Maybe all of my carefully-thought out acrobatics had added up to a big fat zero. Maybe I'd made too many assumptions. I mean, the demons could've been heading anywhere from Nixon. Hell, they could've pivoted and gone straight back to Reno to enter the Demon Bazaar. I walked in the fresh breeze, my boots sinking rocks into the sand. To anyone else, the lake seemed beautiful. A marvel of the Southwest and a wonder of the state of Nevada. But I could feel the air on my skin and it felt... sticky. Something wasn't quite right in the Pyramid Lake. And it wasn't just the rumors that had sent my imagination to places where it shouldn't have gone. I zipped up my jacket and walked to the shore.

The water lapped at my boots. It was clear and bluish, showing me the rippling bottom and the grainy sand. Unlike my beloved Lake Tahoe, this place felt like a whirlpool, just waiting to grab my midriff. It was all in my supernatural sense, of course—the old gods that lived in my veins. They whispered of dangers in my ear while my human side marveled at the view. My boot slid into the water and I felt a tug.

It wasn't anything physical. My first instinct was to jerk my boot away. I resisted the urge. Deep under my skin, my dragon perked up her scaly head.

Souls. Thousands of them. They glistened beneath the surface of the lake like oil. Human sacrifice was never pretty. It left an ugly stain in the universe. I had never felt so many souls trapped in one place. It was eerie and terrifying. I believed Tick when they told me the story. But now, I felt it in the marrow of my bones. The collective sense of betrayal had trapped the spirits beneath the water. My dragon felt them stir beneath the surface. I swallowed, and almost didn't hear as Tick walked up beside me.

"Brrr," they said. Out of the corner of my eye, I saw they were once again wearing their poncho. They shoved their hands into the front pocket. "This place gives me the creeps and a half. And humans *fish* here?"

My bracelet thrashed against my wrist. "And drown here."

Their eyes went to the shimmering scales on my face. "Whoa."

"Yeah," I said. "My dragon isn't liking this." I didn't add *or is liking it too much.* "Let's move. Maybe there's something down the shore."

We walked down the wet sand, cool wind blasting our cheeks and toward the tufa formation that had given the lake its name. I knew what Tick had meant about Spring in this place. Something about the waking nature must stir the spirits within. That's when the wind carried a sound to me that was a contrast to the Water

Babies' deathly, carnivorous silence. A barking of dogs. Big ones.

My eyes went to the island that sat past the pyramid. It thrust out of the water like a pair of knuckles. Smoke rolled up to the sky.

"What's there?" I asked Tick.

"The Anaho Island," they answered. "No one's allowed there. It's protected by the Paiutes."

"Someone didn't care," I said.

The barking was joined by howling. It was hollow and carrying, as if it was coming from the bottom of a well instead of being carried toward us by water. Every haunting note sank fear into me. Hellhounds.

"I think we found them," I said.

18

I TURNED AROUND TO Tick.

"That's it," I said. "This is where you get off this ride."

They blinked at me. "What?"

Digging into my pocket, I pulled out their seal. "Take it and go."

Head cocking to the side, they took the seal. Their feet stayed planted.

"And you?" they asked.

"I'm gonna go take a closer look," I said. "See how many there are, and locate the souls."

Tick raised their dark eyebrows. Their orange curls bounced in the breeze. "You can't be serious."

I laid a gentle hand on their shoulder. "You've helped me find them. Thank you," I said the last part with utmost sincerity. "But this is the part where I do my job."

"You don't even have your partner," they said. "Aren't you going to call it in?"

My lips were getting dry in the wind. I licked them.

"Yes," I said. "As soon as I can give them a proper head count." Pushing my hair behind my ears, I squinted at the smoke. "What am I supposed to tell them now? I heard some howling?"

The demon spawn shifted from one foot to another. The mage hand grabbed their collar and tugged toward the road. It was clearly the smart one in the relationship. Tick swatted it away.

Head ducking, they glowered at me under dark eyebrows. Their hands dug deeper into the poncho's front pocket. "And what, you're just gonna leave me to hitchhike?"

I shook my head. "If you walk up to the ranger's station, I'm sure he'll be happy to call you a ride."

"And what if he's some kind of molester?" Tick asked in a dramatic tone. "You're gonna just leave me to my fate?"

I squinted at them. "What are you doing? Your debt is repaid. Don't you owe a lot of money to some mysterious organization?"

Tick kicked a stone, and it plopped into the water. "Are you going to make me say it?"

Incredulous, I just stared at them.

"I don't exactly... have anywhere to go." Their mage hand was doing a "cutting off" motion, and I agreed with it. "If you're only going to look at how many there are, then what's the harm?"

Narrowing my eyes, I gave the trickster a long, hard look.

"You're hoping to score some soul husks, aren't you?"

They shook their head so vigorously, their head looked on fire. "No way I'm touching one of those things again. It felt— so wrong. Like... holding a curse in my hands."

"What did you do with the last one?" I asked.

"Buried it," they admitted. "Just let me come. I won't get in the way." When I didn't answer, they dropped their eyes to the ground. "I shouldn't have taken it, like it was some *thing*. My soul could be cursed. I want to make it right."

We stared at each other. The mage hand kept tugging at Tick, but they wouldn't budge. I had a feeling that if I said no, the trickster would follow me anyway. They felt like they carried a karmic debt, and I knew something about that. Plus, my sensibility reminded me that they were scrappy and smart. I could use someone like that on a spy mission.

"Okay," I said finally. "But I'm in charge here. You listen to everything I say. If I say run, you cast your camouflage and you run. We go in and out. The van has two surges left—one to get us on that island, and one to get us back. Deal?"

They nodded and grinned.

"For a thief, you have a serious White Knight complex," I said.

They winked at me. "Only because you're hot."

Together, we climbed back into the van. Tick eyed the shore of the Anaho Island.

"How are we gonna—"

A grin splitting my face, I pushed the surge button.

The van jerked forward with a teeth-rattling speed. The jump didn't have to pierce realities, so I'd only given the button a tap. It was enough to propel us over the water and land us on the shore. The hill of the island now rose above us instead of across a mile long stretch of water.

"Holy Coyote!" Tick mumbled through their fingers. They looked a little green. "I think I'm gonna hurl."

"Not on my clean seats!" I said brightly. "Take it outside."

The shore was empty and silent as the water lapped the sand. I switched gears and drove around the mountainous formation at the edge of the island. The smoke was just up ahead. Thanks to Uncle Ophis, the engine was nearly silent. I got as close as I dared and stopped when I could just see the gleam of the fires.

"Okay," I said. "We stay quiet and low to the ground. Follow my lead."

Together, we crept through the dark and around the rock formation. I don't exactly have night vision, so I really had to watch where I was going. Sage brush and ragged rocks covered the terrain. Tick moved through the dark like they were born to it. The mage hand illuminated their path just enough to not be spotted from a distance. So much for taking the lead. My steps soft, I followed the trickster to the fires. The smoke was coming from the flat part of the island where seagulls were settling in their nests. The howling was louder here. Every time it erupted, my legs wanted to turn us around and run. Good thing we were downwind. Hellhounds were excellent trackers.

When we stopped to regroup, I nodded up a slope. We crawled up rough stone and peered over the ledge.

Rudy had said that fifty devourers had escaped the sinkhole. I don't know where he got those numbers. The actual count made the hair rise on the back of my neck.

"At least a hundred," Tick whispered next to me. "Holy shit."

I agreed. Devourers sat around pockets of fires that dotted the landscape. They were burning sage and driftwood to keep them alight. Hellhounds were lying at their sides. From here, they looked like over-grown hyenas with sparkling red eyes. I gulped.

"Burning fires? This is sacred land, you bastards," Tick growled.

"Talk about colonizers," I said slowly. "These ones aren't even from this realm."

Handy nudged me and pointed at my pocket.

"Right," I said. "Calling it in."

Falling behind the rocks, I dialed Zan's number. He could have the glory of finding them. This was beyond my capability to handle on my own, even my pride knew that. What I needed to do now was save my badge. My call went into a busy signal. Not even a voicemail. I frowned as I stared at my phone and tried again. Nothing. Nada. So much for my plan to leave myself out of this.

I tried Rudy next, no answer. Uncle Ophis must've not found him yet. At least I could leave a voicemail. Keeping it brief, I filled him in on the situation.

"Crap," I whispered. The sky over our heads was turning was a dark blue to a pitch-black. I couldn't waste any more time. It was better to get in trouble than get dead.

I dialed Chief Baran. His pleasant baritone answered right away. Relief rolled over me.

"Chief," I said, "I found them."

"Who?" he asked, voice tense.

I swallowed. "The devourers. I'm sorry, Chief. I followed their trail. But I found them!" I closed my hand over the speaker. "They're at Pyramid Lake. On Anaho Island."

"How many?"

I described what we'd seen.

"And the souls," he asked. "Did you locate them as well?"

"Not yet," I said.

"I'll send an extraction team," he said. "Find the souls."

Blinking in confusion. "I have to leave the scene. I have a civilian with me."

"You brought a civilian?" he demanded. There was a heavy silence on the other end. "Stonefield isn't going to like this, Green."

"I know," I said. "I'm so sorry, sir."

"If you manage to track the souls, maybe I can talk him into letting you keep the badge."

Dragging a hand over my face, I nodded. "Yes, sir."

After hanging up, I looked at Tick who looked back expectantly.

"They're coming," I said.

"We should go back to the van," Tick said, not unreasonably. "Get the shit out of here."

Shaking my head, I began moving again. "I have to find the souls before the extraction team gets here."

They looked at me, incredulous. "And *I* have a White Knight complex?"

"I'm a White Knight professionally," I said.

"Pfft," Tick said. Without another word, they cast camouflage over both of us.

Together, we crawled over the rocks like a pair of spider monkeys. The fires below seemed never-ending. My thighs were burning when Tick's mage hand tugged at my coat. My dragon told me that the souls were nearby. I followed the pull and my bracelet thrashed on my wrist.

"There," Tick said. "Is that what I think that is?"

I looked where they were pointing and pressed my hand to my mouth.

A slithering mass of glistening souls was tucked between the rocks. I couldn't count how many there were. Each one of them a life, stolen from their Underworld. Falling back, I panted.

"Shit."

My dragon roared in my head, loud and demanding. I needed to go back, needed to wait for the rescue. Tick looked panicked. Their lips pursing together, they sank to the ground. I needed to get them out of here.

A pair of devourers waddled over to the mass of souls, their claws dragging. Their appearance made fear prickle over my skin. Hacking and grunting in their coarse language, a devourer fished out one glistening orb. He gobbled it down like he was having a midnight snack. Tossing the husk over his shoulder, he cackled as a hellhound gobbled it up. He grabbed a couple more from the enchanted net they used as storage and started back to the fires with his demon pal.

I saw red. Scales crawled up my arms. Immediately, I knew I couldn't go. Leaving those souls didn't just go against every fiber of my being. It went against the command of my spirit. Screw waiting for the team. These souls had been here for days. Who knows how many lives had already been lost? The dragon swelled inside me. *Take them*, she groaned, *take them!*

Her claws raked under my skin. *They're not supposed to be here. Let us have them. Now!*

Teeth gritted, I clutched at my bracelet. No. We were going to do this *my* way, not hers.

"You should hide," I said to Tick. "I have to do something stupid." To avoid doing something *stupider*, I added silently. If I didn't get those souls out of here, my dragon would burst out of my clothes, bracelet or no bracelet. It wasn't just the devourers I needed to protect these souls—these people—from.

They looked at me for a long time. "Stupider than sneaking around a bunch of hellhounds?"

Not trusting myself to speak, I nodded.

"Then, I'm coming, too," Tick said. "No way I'm hanging around in the dark by myself, waiting to be found."

"Fine," I was beyond reason. "You want to help? Help." My hand drew out my gun, and I handed it to Tick. A ferocious grin flashed across my face. I wondered how much of the dragon was in it. "I know exactly what we need to do."

I found the ERS van in the dark. Without Tick, I was basically blind. Fury made me careless as I crashed through the sage. Luckily, the demons either didn't hear or took me for local wildlife. The dragon swept over my senses, and I clutched my wrist where the bracelet thrashed against the magic of my shifter form. It was a shame I'd wasted a surge to get off Zan's mountain. Surging to the souls and back would've been much safer. Alas, I needed that last bit of juice to get off the island. The space between the rocks was protected by demons from all sides. The only way forward was through. I'd given Tick my gun, but also the easier job. They were to sneak down to the souls and help me shove them into the back once I broke through the throng. I didn't elaborate on how I was planning to get there. It might've been more straightforward than the professional sneak was comfortable with. I told them I'd bring the car around. I just didn't tell them *how.*

I didn't turn on the headlights. Praying I wouldn't hit a rock, I drove in the moonlight to the other side of the hill. The demons were having a great time in front of the fires and didn't see me drive slowly up between the sage bushes and the blades of dry grass. I drove down to the shore where I could see the hill behind and went to the side opposite the soul trap. Since I didn't have stealth on my side, I had to go with the element of surprise.

I could only hope that Tick didn't see me do that and chicken out. Speaking of chickening out. Breathing in through my nose and out through my mouth, I told myself this was like any another rescue mission. I was an ERS rescuer. Who cares if I was after one soul or a hundred? This was a job, and I was good at my job. Snotty valkyries be damned. The dragon helped. She was thrashing inside my skin in a way that made me forget about silly things like my life. Get the souls, get out.

I flipped the stick to "Drive" and pushed the pedal to the metal.

At first, I went without my lights. Then, I flipped them on as I pummeled into the throng of demons waiting their turn in front of the fire. I was rewarded with shrieks and hard bodies flipping over the hood. Their claws scraped the paint as they tried to hang on.

The hellhounds were faster to react. They spotted me as soon as I started hitting their masters. They weren't intimidated by the van. As I gunned past them, I saw why. These damned beasts were five feet at the shoulder. Their spotted hides blinked in and out of the lights of my headlamps. Swerving, I put one on its ass. The other didn't hesitate to try to make an example out of me.

Their claws raked over the hood and sides of the van. I winced at the screeching sound, like fingernails scraping a chalkboard amplified beyond belief. Luckily, the van was tougher than a tank. I just hoped it could withstand the assault of the nastiest doggies in the world. Finally, I was going fast enough past the burning fires to leave them behind.

I gassed toward the hill where Tick had spotted the souls. My arm twisted the wheel to the left until my tires screeched and the back of the van swung around. I hit the switch and the barn doors of the van swung open. The seals pulsed as they sensed untethered souls nearby. I jumped out of the driver's seat and ran to where the doors yawned toward the slithering mass of souls. Up close, they were even more horrific. Glowing soul husks littered the sand.

"You call that "bringing the car around?" Tick demanded. They'd leapt out of the shadows like a wraith. "Are you fucking crazy?"

"Bought us some time, didn't I?" I said.

"Yeah, thirty seconds!"

I ran toward the soul net. "Better move, then!"

Together, we jumped to either side of the glowing cluster. Tick pushed, and I tugged on the souls. They slipped between our fingers, barely solid, but somehow weighing more than a ton of lime rock. Handy was helping, but the three of us were moving slowly. I could see into their depths and swallowed. My dragon wanted them. She wanted them *badly.* I grappled with the desire with all my might. Tears burned hot in my eyes. The van was mere feet away. I was so close.

"Stop," I gasped. "Please don't."

"What?" Tick yelled. I could barely hear them over the barking of hellhounds and the hollering of demons riding them. Twenty seconds.

"Push!"

I made myself focus on the souls. I'd never seen this many contained in one place. A magical net of this strength was something I couldn't imagine. This kind of craftsmanship pointed to another demon, at least a Duke, directly in the command of Lucifer, to pull something like this off.

My fingers felt like the netting would slice right through them. Sweat rolled into my eyes.

"Push!" I roared.

Tick panted. "I can't!"

"You can't die!" I yelled over the noise. "Think of all the festivals you'd miss! Rainbow Gathering! Burning Man!" I breathed in a lungful of smoky air. "Coachella!"

"Fuck Coachella!" Tick screamed.

They pushed so hard, I almost fell backwards. I grinned through my sweat. If we were going to die tonight, it would at least be while cursing the pretentious douches of Coachella.

The barn doors pulsed with energy. The seals hummed inside the van. I knew my seals, and the ERS seals were beautifully wrought. Also, they worked. Every single one of them. The souls responded to the wards pulling them inside.

"I won't hurt you," I said to them. "I will protect you. You will have another chance at life."

The howling drew closer as the hellhounds caught wind of our sweat.

"If I die," Tick panted, "I will haunt you 'til the end of time!"

My laughter was loud and manic, carrying up to the sky. "You won't be the only one!"

Shoulder to shoulder, we pushed the souls into the van. The seals flared a luminescent blue. I fell back as the ERS van trapped its customers inside. I grinned from ear to ear. Slamming the doors closed, I grinned at Tick.

"See?" I breathed. "Easy-peasy—"

"Lemon squeezy!" Tick shrieked.

The demons descended on us.

19

"Gun!" I yelled at Tick.

They were scrappy enough to toss it at me instantly. I caught it mid-air and shot it toward a howl.

The first hellhound descended on top of me, knocking me clear off my feet. The giant, yellow teeth of the creature snapped at my neck. Up close, it was as different enough from Bono as a mountain lion was from a house cat. Its weight bore me down and its breath bathed me in the stench of sulfur. It was pointless to shoot salt into a hellhound. They weren't technically demons, but dogs bred in Hell. Soul husks made them what they were. I slammed the metal butt of the gun into its temple. It did little except to piss it off. The devourer riding atop it cackled a sickening resemblance of a laugh.

I shot him in the face. He screeched, and I rolled out from under his hound.

Expecting a quick retaliation, I scrambled to my feet. A shimmering flash shot past my head and the demon screeched. Handy wouldn't hold him long. What had I been thinking bringing my salt gun? I should've brought a bazooka.

The door to the passenger seat swung open, and I saw the pale oval of Tick's face.

"Get in!" they yelled from the inside.

My boot swung over the threshold. And never landed.

A pair of teeth as big as my head dug into my lower spine. I howled. The hellhound had probably been hiding in the shadows, waiting for the cavalry to arrive. I was flung in the air like a dirty rag. My back hit the ground. I heard Tick scream. The hellhound stomped its paws onto my chest. My gun lay useless by my side. I grabbed for it and couldn't reach it. The paws of the beast had kicked it out of reach. It wouldn't have been effective against this horrible thing, anyway. These hellhounds had been living on husks of souls for days. And now, it was about to rip a fresh one out of my chest. I kicked at it and used my demigoddess strength to push it off me. It was no use. The thing was at least three hundred pounds. I thrashed and gasped as the rough stones beneath tore at the new wounds on my lower back. This was a bleeder.

My dragon uncoiled. It found the living energy inside the hound and *pulled*. The creature whined and fell off me. It darted into the dark. From the distance, I heard Tick calling me. Survival overriding the pain and the fear, I scrambled to my feet. My thighs were growing numb quickly. I stumbled back to the driver's seat. The wound on my lower back didn't actually hurt anymore. I knew, from my experience with supernatural predators, that this wasn't good.

I slid onto the seat and slammed the door closed as more hounds rushed us.

"About time!" Tick barked.

Barely feeling my feet, I pushed the brake and clicked the transmission into reverse. We'd made it, we really had. And now, the souls and the two of us were getting the shit out of here. My headlights pierced the dark as I sped down toward the shore. The surge button gleamed on the dashboard and my finger reached for it.

A figure stepped into the headlights. It was a middle-aged man, wide-shouldered and handsome. I slammed the brakes and the van jerked to a stop.

"Chief," I breathed. Relief made me slack.

Tick narrowed their eyes in suspicion. "Who is that?"

Opening the door, I fell out onto the sand beneath. My legs gave way and Chief Baran caught me.

"Alright, Green?" he asked.

"Chief," I gasped. My legs were more and more immobile with every beat of my heart. Did the hellhound's jaw hit a nerve? "You came!"

I realized I wasn't hearing any more howling. The silence that hung over the island was sudden. It was like someone had muted the TV in the middle of a car chase scene. It felt unnatural. Not that I was complaining. The extraction team must've mowed down the demons. That was fast.

Chief held me by shoulders. I was ready to kiss his scruffy face.

"How bad is it?" he asked as he looked at my wounds. His brow creased in concern. "Can you stand?"

I shook my head, uncertain. My whole back was on fire. "How did you get here so fast?" I asked.

His warm eyes were on me as he wiped the blood off my cheekbone. I hadn't even noticed my face got cut. "I hurried," he said.

I nodded and steadied myself. My head spun from the strain. I must've hit my head pretty hard as the hound slammed me down. A new head injury would make a delightful addition to yesterday's concussion.

"Tick," I said, "this is—"

The trickster wasn't behind me, where I'd expected them to be. The passenger seat of the van was empty. Where had they got to? Suddenly, I was feeling like I'd been drinking all day. Everything went a little loopy.

I tried to focus on Chief's face, but it swam in my vision. "We got the souls."

"Of course you did." He wrapped his arm around my shoulder. "Let's find you somewhere to sit down."

His voice threaded through me like a strong drink. It relaxed me and turned down the pain. Was this some sort of satyr magic?

Walking me closer to the water, he sat me on a rock. He landed in the sand in front of me.

"Why don't we take the van back?" I asked. "Is Astrid here? She can give Tick a ride. The back of the van is full—"

Across from me, Chief Baran smiled. His face was so comforting and familiar. The moon rose over his head. Funny—I'd noticed how handsome he was before, but right now he looked positively hot. It must've been the adrenaline, or the relief of being rescued. Who knew I could appreciate an older man like this? Behind him, the water wasn't still any longer. It was rippling and frothing onto the shore. Something was nagging me in the back of my mind. As soon as I was close to catching *what*, my eyes went to Chief Baran's, and I forgot.

"You care about the souls, don't you, Chrys?" he said. "Really, really care. This was the reason I made sure you kept your job after Hades."

My tongue feeling like cotton, I nodded.

"I—"

He raised his hand. "There is no need to thank me. There was never any need. Talents should be rewarded." His smile was gentle, and it made a soft thrum of wanting to please him hum through me. Where did that come from? "When one is useful, they should be used for their purpose. Don't you think?"

My head swam, and I nodded. How many times had I hit my head in the last twenty-four hours?

"Rescuing summoners from Hell is a waste of your talents," he said. "You know it, and I know it. Wouldn't you like to save innocents? Someone deserving to be saved?"

An echoing noise rose from the water behind him. It sounded like children crying. My dragon perked up her head.

"This lake," the Chief said. I blinked down at him. His words came to me as if through gauze. "Do you feel those souls in the water?"

His eyes swam in the dark and suddenly looked much younger. Brighter. I nodded.

"Yes," I said. "They're strong and they're…" I felt the roof of my mouth with my tongue. I tried to phrase the feeling they gave me when I walked down the shore. It was anger and betrayal, yes, but it was also something else. "Lonely."

He nodded and helped me to my feet. I wobbled a bit, but he threw my arm over his shoulder to steady me.

"It's not right that they're in there," he said. His words were loud in the deafening silence. My dragon agreed. "Why don't you call them? We should take them with us. Release them into the universe."

The dragon tugged at me, and my bracelet thrashed. It really wasn't right that the souls were there and not waiting for rebirth. I could feel their cries in the depth. Heard them grow louder in my ears. All those children that never even got their chance. The loneliness pulled at me. My eyes filled with tears.

I nodded. "Yeah." I said. "Okay."

Saving souls was what I did. And owed the world a few. Maybe saving all those baby souls would fix what I'd broken. Finally, fix everything. The loneliness pulled me toward the water and the Chief helped me walk.

"You'd just need to summon them, like you always do with the souls," he said. "I'll take care of the rest."

This was why they drowned the fishermen, I realized. Because they were lonely. They wanted someone to make them feel like they hadn't been abandoned in that cold, dark water. Scared and betrayed. I dipped my fingers in,

Chief supporting my arm as I crouched. My head pulsed with pain and my vision swam. I could help them. I could save them all.

"Small goat, little goat," I sang in Old Slav, "Come to my stead. Not where, not there, but here instead." The song uncoiled inside of me, and I suppressed the dragon as she wanted out. All she wanted to do was eat those souls, but I wouldn't let her. She strained against my skin. I felt hot and sweaty all over. Their thoughts rippled over my consciousness, and I could hear them weeping in the dark before the water took them. "I will groom you, I will feed you, tie you to a stake. Come to me, to my stead, not there but here instead."

The water rippled as if carried by a breeze, even though the air was still.

"Yes," the Chief said. His voice was unfamiliar, but I was too enthralled by the movement to pay attention. "Bring them to me, Chrys."

I sang the song again. Massive rising and movement lurched out of the water. Tiny figures began rising out. Not quite the babies they once were, but orbs of light that their spirits had left behind. Too pure to have a human form. Ego-less. I raised my hand in the air and felt the scales prickle my skin.

"There you go," the Chief continued. I felt his hand leave my shoulder.

I couldn't count how many rose out of the water. It looked like hundreds. Every single one was a soul that could be reborn. They could have a life again, the babies that never saw their first year on earth. No longer lonely in the deep waters of the Pyramid Lake. They rose all around the island like fireflies. Tears rolled down my face. Near and far. Whispers filled my mind. They were so full of potential, of the people that they never became. Abandoned and betrayed. My chest clenched. My dragon hummed inside of me, and I could feel scales break over my skin.

"That's it," the Chief said over my head. His voice came down to me distorted, and I could feel some sort of change happen in the air. Heat rose behind my back where he stood. My eyes were on the souls, the dragon inside of me refusing to break her slitted eyes away from so many that drifted toward us. They were the most beautiful thing she and I had ever seen.

They swarmed around us. My eyes and my mind were full of them. I thrust out my arms and sank to the ground. Their crying turned to songs and their laughter filled my heart.

I collapsed onto the sand. Water lapped at my wrists and knees, and I didn't even remember getting that close to the shore. We could take them home and toward rebirth. The song went quiet in my chest and I felt purged and my head was ringing.

"Thank you, Chrys," a voice said over my head. I blinked sticky tears out of my eyes. I no longer recognized Chief's voice. Maybe it was the songs of the Water Babies that distorted reality. "I'm so glad I kept you alive all these years."

I froze. The moon danced on top of the waves. Then it disappeared from my view as a shadow fell over me.

Two heads—a bull's and a ram's—leered at me from the right and left shoulder of the man standing over me. The human head in the middle smiled. He resembled Chief Baran in the same way a chimera resembled a garter snake. His face was changing quickly. Hair crawled up his cheeks and his eyes were growing warmer. Fire flickered in his irises. If I squinted, I could still see the Chief and feel my pull toward him. I'd felt that hypnotic charm before. The sedative that was his voice. Lafayette's words dragged through me.

We know their master well. After all, he's our kinsman.

My blood turned to tar in my veins. I felt like a statue, stiff and still, as the realization beat over me like wings. The figure that haunted my nightmares, and the demon that killed my best friend stood over me.

"Asmoday," I breathed.

Lifting myself on my elbows, I looked up at my boss. A man who had put on that handsome, unremarkable human illusion to deceive me and the rest of the Spiral.

"How is this possible?"

He crouched over me. The bull head laughed silently as he pushed hair out of my eyes. The water around me was freezing, but I barely felt it. Asmoday's human face smiled a pitying smile.

"I knew you were special, Chrys. Your father gave you powers that brought me to the human realm." Water Babies danced around us like tiny lanterns in the night. They reflected in the bulging eyes of the bull and the ram. "I've been free all these years. Alas, I could not leave my brethren behind to suffer under Lucifer's rule. When I learned of what you'd done in Hades, I knew that your power was what I needed to liberate my kin. Now, with the power of these innocent souls, I can finally break down the gates of Hell." His hand was warm as it cupped my cheek.

"Thank you."

His chin went up and his mouth opened. Thousands of little lights, of little people, rushed into him.

20

MY DRAGON ROARED INSIDE my chest. It wanted the souls that Asmoday was devouring. I didn't have the strength to control it, but I didn't need it. Cold filled me as my blood left me through the wound on my spine.

It hurt so much. Drawing a shuddering breath, all I could do was watch as the Prince of Demons devoured the souls of these children I'd helped him steal. His head snapped back and everything went still. The black night around us was blinding.

"It's okay, Agent Green," the Chief said in his old voice. "You've come full circle. You have summoned me, and I watched you, protected you." He swelled in size and grew large with the souls stolen and consumed. I had been such a fool. Why would the Chief of Supernatural Defense take an interest in an outcast like me? The only person who could only take an interest in someone so dangerous—so tainted—was someone even more dangerous and tainted than me. "When you ate those souls in Hades, I knew you were more than just a demi by-blow. You were a weapon." He licked his lips as he stared down at me. "Crippled with guilt and gagging for approval. Just like the first time we met, you were just what I needed."

I blinked up at him. "You lured me here tonight," I said. "You knew... you knew I wouldn't just find the souls. I'd go after them."

"Of course. You have repressed the dragon for so long, you're barely containing it. And I need it close to the surface." His smile was gentle. "Your quick thinking almost ruined my plans, though." I saw the souls glow in his mouth. I felt sick. "I couldn't let you leave the island. Only a shepherd like you could call them."

Shepherd?

"*Her*," I corrected him. "My dragon."

His eyes went soft with compassion. I wanted to punch him. Unfortunately, my limbs were filled with ice. "You should be proud," he said. "Someone as insignificant as you could only dream of such usefulness."

The howling was back. I could hear the devourers and hellhounds stir somewhere in the dark. There hadn't been an extraction team, of course. No one was coming. Where was Tick? Were they alive?

"With my army freed, I'll be able to take a chunk of the human world. Things will never be the same." The ram and the bull nodded from his shoulders. "But I'm getting ahead of myself." He looked back at my van parked in the shadows of the hills. "Oh yes, I'll take these back now."

He motioned. I heard the demons descend on it. Claws struck metal and hellhound teeth dug into the doors. I flinched as I listened to my van being torn apart. My and

Rudy's van. I prayed to all the gods whose help I didn't deserve that Tick wasn't still inside.

Asmoday's hand reached out and grabbed me by the neck. He lifted me out of the water. I tried to kick, but my legs wouldn't move.

"I can't believe you came here just for them," his humanoid face looked at me with what was almost pity. "They're filthy human souls made even filthier by their petty human sins."

"Everyone—deserves—a chance," I gasped.

He inclined his human head. "It must be hard for you, being who you are. How many souls did you eat in Hades?" he asked. "Five? At least you will die knowing that you won't hurt anyone else."

His faces blurred in my vision. The animal heads laughed as his eyes slitted into an expression of bliss. He was enjoying killing me. I felt my throat getting crushed. My vision blackened at the edges. When I saw a shimmer behind the demon, I thought my soul was finally ready to join my father.

The familiar click of the salt cartridge sliding into place got my attention. My gun. Shots rang through the air, and Asmoday barked in surprise. His two heads swung back. What flea would dare attack him after his resounding victory?

His hand loosened around my neck. I didn't know what I could do with that, except to fall into the water like a half-dead carp. Luckily, the hands that grabbed me had other plans.

Tick's weedy poncho momentarily smothered me, and I knew exactly which flea had bitten Asmoday.

"Time to show that vagabond hustle, Doll Face," Tick's voice said into my ear.

Behind us, Handy emptied my last salt cartridge into Asmoday. The demon Prince swore and grabbed at the apparition. It would've been funny if I wasn't half-dead and Tick wasn't risking their life to keep me that way.

My legs caught me with an effort and I let Tick drag me down the shore. They were stronger than I expected, their body solid under my weight. Their camouflage spell enveloped us in a sound-muffling cocoon.

There was a sizzle in the air as Handy joined us. Asmoday's barks of rage were drawing further away.

"As much as I'd like to carry you, Princess," Tick said. "I need you to move your ass."

I took a proper look at them. Even in the dark, I could see a black eye. Their poncho had claw tears. While I was stealing Water Babies, they'd been fighting for their life. I moved my ass. It was slow going. I wondered if the hellhound's teeth had nicked a nerve in my spine. My legs could move, but I couldn't really feel them.

We slunk through the darkness that was left by the Water Babies. I wanted to cry, but I moved my feet by drawing on a survival instinct that trumped all the self-blame in the world.

"Find her!" Asmoday roared. "Send the hounds!"

The howling filled the air, and I felt Tick beginning to drag me as they walked.

"Shit!" they panted. "They'll find us in minutes. Get to the water! We'll have to swim for it!"

My breath felt like fire bursting out of my lungs. The hellhounds barked in an excited frenzy. They were coming after us fast.

I pushed Tick into the water, and I turned my body toward the hounds to block the demon spawn. The camouflage spell sizzled into nothing around us. Not that it was helping anymore. The hounds had followed the smell of my blood like footprints in the snow.

"Go! Get to the other side!" I said to Tick. "I'll buy you time."

Shaking, I grabbed a piece of driftwood. I had lost the souls I'd been hunting and fed thousands of innocent souls to a demon Prince. I didn't deserve to get off this island, but Tick did.

I swung the wood around my shoulder like a baseball bat. My legs felt like logs as I planted them wider.

"Bring it, assholes," I snarled.

The leader of the pack landed on the sand in front of me. His pin-prick red eyes looked at me like I was an injured gazelle. Two more hounds joined him on either side. They were going to flank me. I re-gripped my "bat" with sweaty palms. This was going to *hurt*.

A yelp came from the leader. I blinked at his expression. Collapsing like a small avalanche, his body fell to the ground. I wasn't sure who was more surprised—me or the hound. The moon caught a jagged edge of the weapon. Its pointy bit was buried in the hound's jugular. An ulak, thrown with the precision of a surgeon.

Whistling through the air foreshadowed another hit. The hound to my right collapsed with an ulak sticking out of its eye socket. The third snarled as it spun around, looking for the invisible threat. Problem was, the threat really *was* invisible. A hand pulled the first ulak out of the fallen hound's neck. Death's mantle fell off him as the reaper swung the weapon around to open the third hound's throat.

Rudy's skull was glowing white through his skin as he turned to me. My hands went limp, and I dropped the driftwood onto the sand. Behind me, Tick released a string of swear words.

"I'll be damned," I breathed.

"We're all damned, Green," the reaper said. "It's the human condition."

I don't remember us piling up onto Rudy's motorcycle in the dark. When my vision flipped back on, we were already on the shore of Pyramid Lake. The fires coming off Anaho island were dark clouds on the backdrop of the moon. Tick clung to my back, and I had my arms wrapped around Rudy. I had the sense that I'd passed out as Rudy's super bike flew us over the water. The two of them must've kept me upright.

My world felt as though it'd gone topsy-turvy. Several hours ago, I'd finally found the demons that the entire agency has been hunting for days. Now, I'd fed thousands of souls to a demon I'd released into the human world when I was twelve. I didn't feel real inside my skin.

"The van," I said to Rudy. "It's gone."

"I know," he said.

How had I been so gullible? I should've seen Chief Baran for what he was. Should've known that he was manipulating me to his own end. But I didn't want to believe that. Didn't want to think that the one person in the agency that had my back was plotting behind it. Dragging my water-logged phone out of my pocket, I wasn't surprised to see that the power button didn't work. As if reading my mind, Rudy pulled his out.

"You better call Stonefield and tell him what happened," he said.

I nodded. Fingers numb, I found the Director's number.

He picked up on the first ring.

"Agent Mort," he growled. "Did you find her?"

"He did," I said. A long, strained silence stretched. "Sir," I added.

"Green," Stonefield said. For the first time since I'd known him, he didn't sound angry. It was infinitely worse than him yelling. "Make this easy on yourself and turn yourself in."

"What?" I croaked. "Chief Baran—"

"Called and told me everything," Stonefield cut me off. "You lost control and ate all those souls."

My voice was hollow. "I didn't. It wasn't me!"

The Director's voice went into negotiating mode. "If you turn yourself in, we can talk imprisonment. If you don't—"

"I didn't eat those souls!" I protested. "Chief Baran is Asmoday, he's going for the Gates, he'll—"

"Enough!" Stonefield barked. I didn't need to see him to know that fire was bursting out of his mouth and into the receiver. "Chief Baran shouldn't have covered for a dangerous beast, let alone allowed you to be near souls. You have one chance to head straight to the Spiral. If you don't, the demon hunters will be notified. They will hunt you down, and they will *put* you down."

21

"You can't go home," Rudy said over his shoulder as he turned the bike toward the freeway. "That's the first place they'll look." I nodded behind the screen of my helmet. I didn't know why I bothered with a helmet, though. If the demon hunters were after me, my head would roll off my shoulders, stat. "Is there somewhere else we can go?"

I made myself think. "Yes. But we have to stop by my apartment," I said to him. My vision swam with exhaustion and blood loss. "They'll ransack it. Mittens is there."

Whether my head was going to roll on the dirt, I couldn't leave my fur baby behind. I also couldn't think about anything beyond five minutes in the future. If I began thinking about anything else, I'd remember what Stonefield said. I shook and made myself focus on the pain that thrummed through my body. I wondered if I was making Tick's poncho bloody. After a pause, Rudy nodded. The reaper's bike shot through the air like the unholy locomotive that it was. Feeling the bike rumble as he sped up, I heard Tick screech in delight. At least someone was having a good time.

Rudy left us to loiter on the shore of the Truckee River while he went to get my cat. Tick's camouflage kept us hidden until he returned. He handed me the backpack with my ghost kitty inside. Mittens poked his head and gave me a meow. I clutched him to my chest.

"There are ten hunters in the building," he said. "They're armed like they're about to face—"

"A soul-eating dragon?" My voice tried and failed for levity.

Rudy gave me a pitying look. I didn't care for it. "I grabbed some things off your coffee table. It looked like you were working on something, so maybe you need them." I took the stack from his hands. It was the notes I'd taken while trying to find the demons. I'd found them alright.

"Where are we going?" Tick asked. They were scratching the top of Mittens' head.

"My mother's," I said. "If there's a place in the state better warded than her shop, I'd eat my foot."

One perk of having no friends is that no one knew where your family rested their heads. This was quickly becoming an advantage as my imminent demise became more and more of a possibility. Rudy's bike shot us to the shore of Lake Tahoe. The sun was coming up over the Ponderosa pines. The "closed" sign swung off the front of Rainbow Road and Shelly's car was gone. I breathed a sigh of relief. My family was still safe and out of the way. The three of us piled up to the front door. The wards painted over the frame hummed and let me through.

Rudy locked the shop door behind us and drew the blinds. Tick pulled a breath in through their nose. "Now, this is what I'm talking about." Dipping their hands into a basket of cats' eyes and moonstone, they sighed. "A proper hippie den." They opened one eye and scanned me up and down. "Again, how did you become such a square?"

I could barely stay upright, and I was so *cold.* "There's a kitchen in the back," I said to Rudy. He nodded and grabbed me under the arm. I hadn't even noticed I'd started sinking to the floor. Pulling my backpack off, I let Mittens down. He meowed and disappeared in the direction of the shop. Maybe he went looking for ghost mice to hunt.

The kitchen doubled as a resting area and came with a couch, a table, and a fridge. Helping me onto the leather couch, Rudy sank down on the floor. He rummaged out a first aid kit he'd grabbed off his bike. If I knew the reaper, it would have everything but unicorn tears.

"Roll over," he said.

Gritting my teeth over a moan, I did. He tore my shirt off my lower back. His silence told me everything I needed to know as he examined the wound.

"Did Uncle Ophis find you?" I asked.

Rudy humphed. "He did."

"Where were you?" I asked.

"Florida," he said.

I turned my head to face him. "Are you serious? You *did* take a tropical vacation?"

He shrugged. "Does this hurt?" Pain blazed up my back, and I gasped. Frowning, he pulled out a purple vial and uncorked it. "Hellhounds' saliva is poisonous. It causes paralysis."

My chest unclenched a bit. "Is that why I couldn't feel my legs?"

"Most likely."

So, it wasn't a nerve. That was a bit of a relief. Maybe I could run a couple of miles before the demon hunters chopped me into mutton.

"You shouldn't stay here," I said. "You should take Tick and go. It's not too late to plead ignorance. Purgatory would be happy to have their darling back."

He uncorked the bottle and sniffed the contents. The smell of vinegar filled the kitchen.

"You don't have to go down with me," I pressed.

"Are you done?" he asked. "I will not let those idiots on the executive panel tell me what to do." He poured the purple liquid onto the gauze and pressed it to my spine. A howl erupted from my throat as my whole body spasmed. Feeling was back in my legs, alright.

Tick's worried face peered over the couch. Rudy kept dabbing and my howls turned to moans. The demon spawn's smile was wry.

"I'll have what she's having," they said.

When Rudy was done, he bandaged the wound. I sat up in my bra and sank into the cushions. The reaper boiled water and pressed a cup of tea into my hands. A tiny green cloud foamed over the top. I recognized a healing potion we'd kept in the van. My lower back throbbed, but I was feeling in one piece.

I smiled. "You make quite the nursemaid."

His handsome face was impassive, but I could see his mouth tilt up just a touch. Grabbing a blanket from a chair, he slid it over my shoulders.

"And you're a terrible patient."

"If you keep being this nice to me, I'll have to rethink us being pals," I said drowsily.

I don't remember when I'd fallen asleep, but when I woke, Rudy was gone and Tick was curled up on the opposite side of the couch. Handy rested on their shoulders. The familiar smells of the shop made me wake up confused. What was I doing at Mom's? Then, the memories coursed through me, and I wished I'd kept on sleeping. I wasn't cold anymore—whatever Rudy had put in the tea had warmed my blood—but I shook with chills. Now that I was rested, my brain caught me up on all the fuck-ups of the last 48 hours. My teeth gritted until I tasted blood. What had I done?

Feeling me wake up, Tick stirred. They stretched, and I heard joints pop.

"How are you?" they asked. Their own face was less puffy and the nasty purple bruise had faded to yellow.

"Just great," I said.

"Really?" Their smile was wide and goofy. "Oh, *that's* good."

I didn't reply. Hands drawing the blanket closer over my shoulders, I stared at the floor.

"You should go," I said. "They'll find me eventually."

"Who will?" they asked. At my confused look, they smoothed down their orange locks. "The demons? The demon hunters? The mother-clucking CIA?" They grinned. "Maybe they'll meet up on the way and kill each other."

"My dragon is a monster," I said. "If I hadn't pulled those souls, Asmoday wouldn't be on his way to Hell. I should've let the devourers take them."

Tick threw their arms over their head. "Is that what you really think?" They sighed in satisfaction at my silence. "Figured as much."

"What should I have done?" I asked. "Let them be sucked down like juice packs? But I made it *so* much worse." Rubbing my face, I shuddered. "And now Asmoday is going to break through the Gates."

Again, I'd played right into Asmoday's hand by escaping. He'd called Stonefield and now the agency was too busy looking for me to pay attention to the Gates. They needed to hunt down the monster, the *Nidhogg*, the Soul Devourer. I bet Astrid was tinkling with excitement.

Tick picked lint off their poncho as if considering something. It still had smears of my blood on it. When they spoke up, their voice was quiet.

"You know how I didn't tell you about my father?" they asked. I nodded. "Well, he died. It was the cops, they shot him."

"Tick—" I swallowed. "I'm so sorry."

They shrugged. "It was my fault. This was before I knew Handy was out of control because I didn't want him. We got pulled over, and he just kept messing with the cops, pulling their badges and shit. It wasn't the first time he was trying to get my attention, but I always ignored him, thought he was bad luck. The cops got scared and started shooting. Pops was trying to protect me." The haunted look in Tick's eyes came and went. They gave me a wobbly smile. "I should've trusted that Handy was a part of me. You know?" They hugged themselves and leaned into the shimmering mage hand as it patted his head. "Maybe he'd still be alive."

"You don't blame Handy?" I asked.

They looked at me like I cussed out their mother. "Of course not! It's his nature. Can't blame someone's nature. It's when you go against it that people get hurt. Gotta trust it, you know?" Clicking their tongue, they looked over the damage on their poncho. "Point is, you're not the only one with regrets." Their face creased, then brightened as they moved to more pressing concerns. "Is there anything to eat around here?"

Dressed in my mom's Blind Melon T-shirt, I sat on the back porch of the store that faced the RV she shared with Shelly. My beloved Crystallizer van sat in the garage ahead. Spread open, my backpack sat in front of me. What they said pulled through me like a thread tied to my core. Trusting your nature. That's not something I'd done in a long time. Not since I was a kid in the back of my mother's van. All my nature has ever brought was destruction to everything it touched. Or did it? I thought about how Asmoday had called me a "shepherd." What happened to "devourer?" This was confusing to think of now. The Demon Prince was going to the Gates, ready to take them down. Devourers, and even more vicious demons, were ready to swarm the earth. My thoughts stumbled over themselves. The Spiral didn't believe me, and my van was gone. What could I do?

To keep my hands busy, I dug out the stack of notes from my apartment. Tick's seal was already back with its owner. Most of the others were useless now. Maybe I could see if—

A piece of paper slid out of the map. It flapped in the wind and moved across the stones before I stepped on it with my boot. I stretched it between my fingers.

"An exciting opportunity lies ahead of you," I read out-loud and snorted. My world might've turned upside down in the last few days, but fortune cookies continued to be bullshit. My eyes went back to the garage, and I froze. They *were* bullshit. It wasn't about what was written in the fortune. It was about the man who'd given it to me.

Rudy stepped outside the shop and walked toward me. He stopped when he saw my expression.

"What?" he said. "What happened?"

"Oh, you know, the usual. Realizing that I'm out of my mind," I said. My eyes went to the reaper who blocked out the sun with his lanky frame. "I know how we can stop Asmoday."

22

WE RAIDED MY MOM'S RV for whatever was in the fridge. Sliced cheese, ham, and fresh strawberry preserves went a treat with sourdough bread. I'd made us a fresh pot of tea. Tick had brought incense from the storefront and lit it around the kitchen. The three of us sat on the ground with the food spread out in front of us. This felt less like planning the dumbest infiltration in history, and more like a picnic. I'd scored a packet of hot sauce from the bottom of mom's freezer and dripped it onto my ham sandwich.

"The point is, we don't have our van," I said. "But it doesn't mean that we can't *make* a van. *My* van, the Crystallizer. This is where Uncle Ophis comes in. All he needs to do is the same thing he does in ERS—make it capable of traveling the metaphysical railways to Hell."

Rudy eyed his bread skeptically. "Do you think he'll make it for you?"

I shrugged. "Uncle O likes a project. And this will be a *project*."

"What about the Spiral?" he asked. "Isn't he required to report you?"

At this, I actually laughed. "Aren't *you* required to report me? He is the Universal Plumber. He was ancient before the Spiral was but a glimmer in the bureaucrats' eyes."

The reaper considered this. "Say that it works. What happens next?"

I leaned back. Making my voice casual, I said: "I summon Asmoday back to Hell."

Tick choked on their tea. "Are you bonkers?"

"I summoned him to the human world," I said, hoping I sounded reasonable. "Why can't I summon him back to Hell? My seals *work*," I added. "Every time."

"This is insane, Chrys," Rudy said. "Even for you."

I nodded. "I know." The green tea was bitter on my tongue and I drank deeply. "Doesn't mean that it won't work."

Handy waved at me, and Tick asked, "So, what do *I* do?"

I dripped some hot sauce directly onto my tongue and shuddered at the pleasant burn. What would it take to keep the demon spawn out of my mad plan? Probably a meteor striking the shop and killing us all.

"You'll provide camouflage for the van," I said finally. "If you're planning to stick around, that is."

They grinned at me. "I'm raking up enough karmic points for two bank robberies over here."

At least someone had their priorities straight. "Can your spell stretch over the van?"

They nodded.

"Well," I dusted the crumbs off my fingers. "Nothing to it but to do it."

Rudy gave me a dark look from his place on the floor. "I still think this is insane and will get us all killed."

I smiled at him. "I know."

Outside, I used Rudy's phone to call Uncle Ophis. His gravelly voice answered, sounding like it came from the bottom of a well.

"Chrysoberyl," he said. "You're in one piece, Veles' Daughter."

I didn't ask how he knew it was me. This was Uncle Ophis, after all.

"For now, anyway," I said. I plucked at mom's shirt, suddenly nervous. What if he refused? Yav would be on fire, and I would be left hiding my ass in demonic In-Betweens for the rest of my natural life. Which would be awhile. "I need a huge favor."

There was a smile in his voice. "What favor can you possibly need from an old Greek?"

I swallowed. "A universal one."

Briefly, I told him about Asmoday and his plan to break down the Gates. He didn't seem surprised that the "Whipper-Snappers" of the agency didn't believe me and were coming after me instead. Like I said, an ancient being like him cared little about "executive decisions."

"I'll be there soon," he said. "Use the reaper's phone to send me your location."

"Thank you! I'll text you the address. Do you need a ride?"

"A ride!" He chortled. "Hestia's tits!"

The line went dead. Grin wide, I pumped my fist in the air. Things were finally coming up, Chrysoberyl.

An eagle cry sounded overhead. I barely had time to look up before three shadows soared over the courtyard in front of my mom's RV. Three giant eagles dive-bombed me.

"Ohhh, shit!"

Turning on my heel, I bolted toward the shop. My mom's wards could hold them off for a while. I didn't know how long, but it was my best chance. I was officially out of time. The Spiral had found me and sent their best hunters—the Hrom brothers. I was five feet away from the door when a shape fell onto the gravel before me. The force of it sent pebbles and dust exploding into the air. Zan stood between me and the door. Perun's axe was sparking in his hands and his eyes were the gray of lightning clouds. He swept out his weapon and electricity charged through my hair. Forget hiding in In-Betweens. I was getting fried, right then and there.

His voice boomed, magnified by the thunder overhead.

"What are you doing here?" he demanded. "You have to run!"

My adrenaline didn't quite catch up with my brain. Pivoting right, my body coiled up to spring toward my mom's RV and the protective wards within. I stopped in my tracks. Looking up at Zan, I saw his expectant face.

"Well?" he said. "Come on, get on my back, let's go!"

Jaro and Rad landed on either side of me. Their spears glinted in their hands.

"Chrys," they said in unison.

Rad stepped toward me. His face looked like he hadn't slept in days. "We've looked all over for you. Are you okay?"

I looked back at Zan in confusion. "You're not... here to kill me?"

The clouds in his eyes cleared. "Kill you? Why in the thunder would I kill *you?*"

Rudy burst through the shop door. His ulaks drew a wide arc in the air. I threw up my hands.

"Stop!"

He hesitated, teeth bared. His eyes went to Zan. There was a flicker of irritation in them I couldn't quite place. Usually, the reaper was a palace of indifference. Why would Rudy have a problem with the Spiral's finest?

"Apparently," I said slowly. "They aren't here to kill me." I turned to Zan. "Right?"

Sliding his axe into a sheathe at his hip, Zan crossed his arms over his chest. He stared at me with an intensity that made me want to kiss him or punch his jaw. Both options had their appeal.

"I know you didn't mean to eat those souls," he said. "This is my fault for not trusting you. The other hunters are staking out the city, but I knew you wouldn't be there. I... remembered you telling me about this place." He looked sheepish. The only time I could've told him about my mom opening Rainbow Road was ten years ago. We were probably naked. This was the wrong image to have in my head. I raised my eyebrows at him. He thought I'd eaten the souls and came to save me anyway?

"One," I raised my finger. "I didn't eat those souls."

"Oh," he said.

"Two," I raised the second finger. "Chief Baran is—"

"I'm sorry," Zan said.

"You're what?" Jutting a pinkie into my ear, I pretended to clean it. "Come again?"

Zan didn't laugh. "I'm *sorry*," he repeated. "I should've been open with you to begin with. When I tried calling you back, your phone was dead. I didn't know what happened to you." He looked genuinely worried, which made me a little uncomfortable. Zandro Hrom regretting his actions? Now, *that* was enough to give a girl a heart attack. He paused. "What about the Chief? Where is he?"

"Well," I said, "to answer your question: Chief Baran is at the Gates of Hell trying to break them down."

His eyes widened. "What?"

"I suppose I should open with telling you that the Chief isn't 'the Chief' at all. He's a demon Prince I summoned when I was twelve." The three Hrom brothers looked at me like I'd just told them the sky was green. I crossed my arms over my chest. Man, were they in for the shocker of a lifetime.

Uncle Ophis was as good as his word. As soon as I was done catching up the brothers, Rudy perked up his head.

"Someone else is here," he said.

I allowed the wards to let the Universal Plumber past the gate and into the courtyard. Ophis Lamprou walked up to us like he just happened to stumble upon the most curious of places in the middle of an afternoon stroll. He carried a Starbucks cup in hand. His moustache drooped on both sides of the cup as he took a sip. Frowning at the taste, he walked up to me.

"Is this what they call tea in this village, Veles' daughter?" he asked. Mumbling, he drank down the brew. It looked scorching hot. When he was done, he crushed the cup between his palms and stuffed it into the pocket of his overalls. It disappeared without as much as a bulge.

"Is he okay?" Tick murmured behind me.

"Oh, yeah," I said, my grin wide. "He is absolutely brilliant."

On the way to the garage, Uncle Ophis took his time admiring the wards Shelly had engraved on my mother's RV. I swelled with pride. My mother's work was nothing to sniff at.

The van greeted me in the dusty silence like an old friend. I patted the purple hood.

"Hey girl," I swear I could feel the metals vibrate under my palm in greeting. "Ready for another adventure?"

I climbed into the driver's seat and started the engine. Pressing down on the gas pedal felt like scratching an itch so deep I forgot it was there. Together, my darling van and I drove out into the sun.

Uncle Ophis pushed his glasses up his nose and I climbed out. Rudy eyed the Crystallizer with all its mushroomy painted glory.

"This is the van you want to take to hell?"

I patted the hood lovingly. "This baby has seen more miles than your entire generation of soul takers."

"By the grace of the Christian God, most likely," he said.

"Try Oberon," I grinned. "My mom is of fae blood."

"Of course she is," Rudy smiled. "What kind of a mutt are you?"

Thumbing my chest, I replied in a drawl: "The 'Merican kind'."

I tossed the keys to Uncle Ophis. At a speed that made all of my joints hurt, he grabbed the bumper and disappeared under the car. Clanking and wrestling came from under it. I didn't remember seeing the man bring any tools. Then, I remembered the paper cup disappear into his pocket. Did he have his own mini-dimension in his overalls?

"Can you do it?" I asked. "Will it go between dimensions?"

"Only if you stop asking insignificant questions, Veles' Daughter," came a muffled reply.

I shrugged and left him to it. The Hrom brothers were discussing something in hushed voices. Zan gave me a loaded stare that made it tempting to read into his sudden appearance. I swallowed.

"Come on," I said to Rudy. "Let's check the shop for protective goodies."

Tick followed us inside and stuck their nose into the teas.

"Does she have any love potions here?"

I snatched a box of expensive tea from their fingers.

"Like you need any," I said. "I bet you already have some horned little babies running around somewhere." I hesitated as I thought about it. "If that's physically possible, I mean."

They winked. "Wouldn't you like to know?"

Digging through my mom's drawers, I found a Dara Celtic knot necklace. I swung it over my head and felt the hum of energy waft over me. Couldn't hurt. Rudy dipped his ulaks into blessed water. Uncle Ophis was still busy with Crystallizer when the canopies of pines turned amber in the setting sun. I figured it was time to do the thing I'd been putting off.

I walked up a moss-covered path snaking up behind Mom's RV. I hadn't made this track in over ten years. Finally, I came across three stones placed on top of each other. I swallowed. My saliva was thick inside my mouth. Using a hand rake that I brought from my mom's garden, I dug into the dirt in front of the pile.

The demon book was sealed in a plastic bag. I dragged the tab open. My fingers seemed to burn as I pulled out the text that was abandoned by Rainbow Dreads all those years ago. The reason why Lizzy was dead. That was a funny transition, I thought in the back of my mind; I no longer felt like it was entirely my fault. Sliding the vile thing under my coat, I walked back to the shop.

Uncle Ophis greeted me with a tired smile. The setting sun colored his bare shoulders in crimson and his overalls looked less cartoony and more like a priest's garb.

He was wiping his greasy hands on a rag. Everyone else had gone inside. I looked at the Universal Plumber as if seeing him for the first time. The dark pooling at his feet slithered. His glasses were pushed on top of his head and the eyes that squinted at me looked their age—thousands of years old.

"She's finished," he said and stuffed the rag in his pocket. "Her body isn't as hardy as the Spiral's vans, but she has spirit. She will carry you where you need to go." My keys appeared in his hand.

I reached for them. "Thank you—"

He held them just out of my reach. "There's something you need to know first."

When I went back to the shop, Zan was waiting for me. Rad and Jaro stood behind him like sentinels.

"We want in," Zan said. "Whatever you're planning, we want to come, too."

I gripped the keys, my heart still hammering after my conversation with Uncle O.

"Are you sure?" I asked. "I don't think you realize what a bad idea this is."

He shrugged. "I trust you. Do you trust me?"

I bit my lower lip. His eyes held mine, demanding an answer.

"To Hell and back?"

23

Uncle Ophis did right by the Crystallizer—her engine ran smooth and her wheel responded in my hands like I'd bought her yesterday. My palms were sweating on the wheel as we rolled down the streets of Reno. We weren't exactly inconspicuous—a purple van with crystals and mushrooms painted on the sides was an eye-catcher. I just hoped that the demon hunters weren't expecting me to roll into town in a circus wagon.

Tick was sandwiched between me and Rudy in the front. Zan and his brothers had crammed themselves in the back. Just remembering their faces as they sat on the benches lined with green faux fur cheered me up a bit. I licked my lips and hit the surge button.

At first, everything went black. Then, like bleach being poured on a black T-shirt, the world went splotchy beige. Floating clumps of dirt swooshed past us and we weren't driving on asphalt anymore. I evened out the van on the bumpy surface of the World Tree root.

The root system is complex and stretches across the bottom of the universe like a mycelium network. It branched out over our heads in a system of dirt-dripping vines. I didn't see an end to it. There may not even be one. In front of us, roots both large and small dropped down into a depth incomprehensible to the human mind. We sat on just one of them, a bug crawling on a thousand-year-old oak.

Luckily, the Universal Plumber had done exactly what I'd asked—the surge had taken us straight to the Gates.

My mom's ancient GPS flashed, and the panel read: "Welcome to Hell."

There was a flickering at the bottom of the root we sat on. Embers glowed and I could already smell the sulfur. I switched the van to drive. We plummeted down the root like tipping down in a roller coaster cart. My stomach went to my throat as the clumps of dirt and root branches whooshed past my vision. The familiar thrill came and went. It was entirely possible that this would be my last trip to Hell. Rudy didn't need to know that, so I gave him a confident smile over Tick's swearing.

Uncle Ophis' expression flashed in my memory. It wasn't pity, exactly, but the face of a General giving a soldier a gun with only one bullet to face an army. A grim understanding of the odds.

"She can only handle one surge," Uncle Ophis said. "You'll only be able to go through the Gates once."

I'd licked my lips, the full implication of it settling into my bones. If I summoned Asmoday in Hell, I'd be trapped down there with him.

"Do you still want it?" he'd asked.

It took me a moment, but my hand didn't tremble as I reached for the keys. "I summoned him," I'd said. "I'll be the one to take him back."

Now, that surety had fled as I heard the horns and the howling of hellhounds. We drove up the familiar curve that overlooked the Gates. I nodded at Rudy.

"Ready, partner?"

No longer hidden, his skull glowed white under his skin. He nodded.

What we saw below was an army. Devourers and hellhounds dotted the width of the root leading to the Gates. They weren't the only ones. I could see succubi cracking whips and pursons, the lion-headed demons of the Mojave Desert, belching fire. Asmoday seemed to pull more than just the demons of gluttony from the depths of Hell. They all wanted a slice of the glory. The Gates themselves yawned open with a flaming, disfigured skull at the top. They were made of charred femurs twining their way up the giant frame. Charming. Inside, I could glimpse a staircase that led further down.

In the middle of the swarm was a three-headed figure. Just looking at him made my chest tighten. It wasn't all fear, though. The bastard took my best friend, and then he came for my life and city. Damn right I was angry.

I leaned back and knocked on the back of the van. The barn doors swung open, and it rocked as three male bodies climbed out. Crouching, they flanked the sides. I rolled down my window and looked down at Zan. The son of Perun looked collected and *hungry*. His axe sparkled at his side. Every line of his body vibrated in anticipation at the sight below.

"Now," I said, "I appreciate the enthusiasm, but remember that you can't go past the Gates. Your presence can be interpreted as an act of war."

He nodded and gave me a thirsty grin. Feathers were already sprouting down his arms. "Plenty of things to do outside."

From the other window, I could see Jaro and Rad bump fists at the sight below. I shook my head.

"Just give me an opening," I said to Zan. "We'll be right behind you. Remember, the big demon with the three heads is Chief Baran. He has a bull, a ram, and a human head. Can't miss him." He nodded, and I swallowed down nerves. "Be careful?"

For a second, I thought he was going to laugh. His smile dropped at my expression and he nodded, serious. "You, too, Chrys."

I nudged Tick and nodded. "Let's do this."

The camouflage spell crackled around us and eagle cries pierced the air. Three giant birds swooped down at the horde and I pressed the gas pedal.

I'd never seen the brothers do their thing before. Watching them drop down from the sky and onto a horde of demons looked like something out of an action flick with a huge CGI budget. In seconds, they were men again. Zan's axe swept out in an electrifying arc and split a devourer into two smoking halves. Grinning ferociously, he leapt at the next one. For a guy that large, he was shockingly fast. Jaro and Rad's spears took out two hellhounds while dodging the fire out of a purson's mouth like they were born to evade it. They blasted through Asmoday's troops like a wrecking ball.

Tick whooped next to me. "Hot damn!"

I agreed. But the demons didn't take long to react to this new threat mowing down their number. Barking and howling, the hellhounds descended on the brothers with devourers riding their backs. It didn't matter, the three of them moved like an army of their own. I stopped gawking and drove after them. Their strategy looked like chaos, but the space they opened was very much deliberate. Wheel in hand, I drove over the root of the World Tree that led to the Gates. Ember flared in front of me and my eyes caught out the yawning opening to the Abrahamic Underworld.

Over the heads of other demons, I saw Asmoday. It was still awful to know that Chief Baran's face was just a mask. The hairy mug between the two animal heads was the demon's true visage. His tail swept around him as his features contorted into fury at the sight of Zan.

"What is this?" he demanded.

Zan gutted an oncoming devourer and turned to see his former boss. His white teeth bared.

"Chief," he said.

"Zandro Hrom," Asmoday growled. "So, you figured out the truth. Never took you for a free thinker." His arms went out. "Leave this place, son of Perun. This is Hell's business."

Zan held out his axe. "You made it my business when you involved ERS operatives."

The Prince of Demons howled with laughter. "You mean agent Green?" He broke off and stared at Zan with new curiosity. "Veles is Perun's mortal enemy. You know what happens in a few *very* short years, don't you?"

I frowned as I waited for Zan to answer.

"What the shit are you doing?" Tick hissed at me. A trickle of sweat formed on their temple. "I'm barely keeping it together, Drive!"

Stepping on the gas, I realized it didn't matter what Asmoday meant. After today, he'd be trapped and I would most likely be dead. Those "few short years" were further shortened to a blip. The camouflage flickered around us. The Gates were several feet away. It was important that we weren't seen. Throwing one last glance at Zan, I sped toward the entrance. Sorry, Hrom.

The last few paces were free of demons. The protective shields flared red over the bony frame of the Gate. It felt the presence of my van. The familiar vibration of the Gate opening for Uncle Ophis' magic made my stomach unclench just a tad. I looked at Rudy. He was poised like a spring, ready to handle whatever waited in Hell. I had other plans.

"Is this—?" Tick breathed.

"Yes," I said. "And this is where the two of you get out."

"What?" they said. Handy landed on their shoulder. "We came to help."

"And you did." I sped up. The sound of the battle behind was nearly deafening. "And now you're going to help yourself."

Rudy's stare almost stopped me from saying my piece. I swallowed and pushed on.

"This is the last favor I ask of you," I said. "This van only has one surge."

His eyes dilated with understanding as he stared at me. "You mean—"

"Yes," I said. "Take Tick. Use the mantle to hide the two of you until Asmoday is inside the Gates. Then, get out with the brothers."

Skull flaring, he glared. "I will not leave my partner behind."

"What about your duty?" I pointed at the trickster, who looked between us, bewildered. "They are a civilian. Take them to safety."

I was playing dirty, reminding him of what was our real job, but I was right. We both knew it. If there was no safe way to get out of Hell, he had to save Tick first. Not me.

Rudy stared at me. There was an expression on his face I'd never seen before. Fear. Fear for *me*.

"Absolutely not," he said. "You turn this van around now."

I jerked the wheel right and pushed the buttons that made his door swing open. "Go!"

Using the momentum, I shoved Tick out the door.

"Now, wait a goddamn minute!" they squawked before they pummeled into Rudy.

Grinning, I blew them a kiss.

"Live another day to hate Coachella!"

Before he fell out, Rudy gave me a look that made me think that if I lived, I'd never stop hearing about it. If I lived. That was a big 'if.' He was too dexterous to fall on his ass and landed in a graceful crouch. That was before Tick fell on top of him. After a moment's scramble of limbs and some very colorful language, Rudy grabbed them by the scruff of their neck. I caught his eyes through the window and gave him a brief nod. He seethed. I didn't give him a choice. He'd resent me for it, but he'd do what needed to be done. In seconds, they were gone. Rudy might not be able to camouflage the whole van but when he went invisible, it was true invisibility. Tick would be safe.

My head was clear for what seemed like the first time in years. To the sound of Asmoday roaring over the screeches of demigod eagles, I pushed the pedal to the metal. The Crystallizer burst through the Gates of Hell.

24

I LANDED IN A desert. No sage brush, no mountains, and no white, cracking surface was in sight, though. Hell greeted me with wind-swept dunes. The sand beneath my wheels was the color of rust, and the sky was the color of watered-down blood. I swung the door of the van open and my boots stamped the sand.

Searing wind picked up my hair and my skin immediately felt stripped of moisture. It was as if the air itself wanted to suck everything it could out of me. After the rage of the battle, the silence was deafening.

Gaping limestone mouths contorted as they gaped up at me from the sand. They seemed less carved out of something, and more like they'd grown from the agony embedded in the dirt. Each one of them was a devourer's nest. This was where we'd rescued Tony three days ago. It seemed like a lifetime. The rotting smell of sulfur crawled down my throat. My Red Bull was cold in my hand and I took a sip. If I was going down, this is the way I wanted to do it—with the Crystallizer as my steed and caffeine as my magic potion. The rotten egg smell was a bummer, but you can't have everything. Out of habit, I checked the salt cartridges on my belt. They wouldn't be much use, of course. At least my gamble had paid off—the devourers were gone. All of them had gone to join Asmoday's army. I wondered if he already knew what I'd done. I hoped not. I wanted the next step to be a surprise, and to see the shock on that bastard's face. Taking the summoning text, I put it on the sand. I picked up a rotting piece of wood—or maybe it was bone, who knew in Hell—and got to work.

The seal came as easily to me the second time as it did the first. Ancient symbols that weren't to be glimpsed by mortal eyes promised riches, sex, and the world at my feet. If only I'd originally cast the seal, and not the summoning. I wanted to laugh and cry at the same time as every line I drew came out perfect. Lizzy would approve.

Words of summoning slithered out of my mouth. I felt my dragon's head pulse out of my chest. This time, she didn't have to correct any mistakes. I'd wanted the seal to work. Contrasting the orange sand, blue light filled the lines. The magic smoldered in the air and azure flames danced over the symbols.

It didn't take nearly as long this time. Roars of devourers and the screams of the succubi accompanied the three heads that rose, shaking with rage, through the seal. The summoning had plucked Asmoday from the midst of the battle. By the sound of it, it wasn't going so great for the demon army. This would be my cue to jump back into my van and surge back to Yav. But there was no surging. No escape.

Asmoday's body rose over the seal, seven feet tall. He threw out his arms as if to balance himself. The ram's nostrils flared and the bull's head shook its horns as it surveyed their new surroundings. Between the animal heads, his humanoid face was full of rage and confusion as he glared at the blood-colored sky. His serpent tail whipped around his legs, one hoofed and one human. For a second, his human face didn't look human at all—it was the human version of the monstrous animals that were attached to his shoulders. Fury twisted his features as he landed on the sand of Hell. He was covered in blood and I was afraid to think whose blood this was. Zan—

He dragged his tail over the seal as if erasing it would mean that he could go back to assailing the Gates. There was no going back. I closed the book with a snap.

"Hi Chief," I said. My voice didn't tremble. "You owe me wishes."

The entirety of his body turned toward my voice. The hair on his chest puffed as the three heads pierced me with all the fury of Hell. His hands grew into claws and his human eyes blazed with murder. He didn't need an army to tear me apart. Suddenly, the fear was back, and I felt my feet slide backwards.

"Veles' daughter," he snarled. "You will die for this!"

My hand flew to my gun, and before I knew it, I was firing at him. He didn't even flinch. The seals crackled as he stepped over them, as if stepping down from a throne. His tail swept me off my feet. He towered over me. The horns pierced the top of his head like broken, black branches. What was left of humanity fled his features and his mouth yawned open to reveal vicious teeth. I saw a blue glow in his throat. The souls he'd devoured. His chins grew to a point and his eyes grew into slits. The succubi blood yielded to a more demonic form.

"I will eat your heart," Asmoday roared. "How dare you bring me back?"

His tail crushed my windpipe, and my vision reddened. My gun raised in my hand and I aimed at his face. He roared as I unloaded a cartridge of salt into his eyes.

When he swept his head back around, his voice was thick with fury, not pain. "You insect! You little half-human whore!" Swelling in size, he blocked out the sky. He was over nine feet tall now and he dwarfed me into the sand. Red saliva dripped from the corners of his monstrous mouth. The horror of him filled my vision and finally, I got a glimpse of Asmoday that no longer had any use for the half-mortal child who had summoned him. "I will tear out every muscle in your body and split every bone! I will boil your intestines!" His breath stank of death and blood. The ram and bull's eyes were blind and rolling, and somehow, they were even more terrifying than his humanoid head. "Is this what you came to face me with?" A hand ripped the gun out of my hand, and he squeezed it in his grip. The metal crunched and the salt pellets dotted the sand. "A toy and a magic book?"

His claw found my ribs and began pushing down. I knew he was as good as his words—he would tear out my heart and eat it. My vision was beginning to blink out, and I made myself re-focus.

"No," I choked out. "Not— exactly."

Scales burst up my arms. I swung my wrist to my mouth and caught the chord between my teeth. Grinding down, I ripped off my mother's protective bracelet.

Without it, my hand felt naked. It felt raw. The surge didn't come from the van this time. It came from inside me. My vision cleared and suddenly I felt *too much.* Like I was too big for my clothes, too big to fit under Asmoday's claws and his fury. My horns, one whole and one broken, pierced through my hair and I used my soon-to-be-gone human face to give the Prince of Demons a toothy grin.

"I brought a friend."

My clothes ripped, and my body swelled. The ground shrank under me. Luminescent coils stretched over the rust-colored ground. Asmoday stepped back, his monstrous face betraying a glimpse of surprise. I was all scales and smooth, long muscle. My muzzle rose in the air. My six claws planted into the sand. Opening my mouth, I let out a good, long roar.

Asmoday's face contorted. What was left of his lips pulled back to reveal his jagged teeth. My head rose to the level of his chest, and I showed him *my* teeth.

"So, this is the big plan," he snarled. "To summon your lizard to fight the Prince of Hell. Who are you to challenge me?" His mouth opened, and I saw Water Babies swirl in its depth. If my human self could barely stand it, my dragon thrashed in fury. She—I—beat her tail against the ground. Asmoday swelled as the blue glow of a thousand innocent souls filled his essence. He was using them to power up. Spikes shot out of his back. His arms grew muscled and his animal heads were now fanged. Throwing out his arm, he made a fist. A sword grew out of his hand. It was as wide as my human thigh and at least four feet long. With a flick of his wrist, flames burst out along its length. "Taste the wrath of a god."

I snapped my jaws and charged at him. His sword drew a flaming half circle.

Stopping mid-lunge, I used my momentum to swing my tail around. My dragon body felt disorienting. There was so much of me. The only time I'd used my scaly form before this was to swim in it. Still, while Asmoday stood taller in the shoulders, I had the advantage of mass. My side crashed into him and I temporarily lost sight of the Prince as my coils buried him down into the desert sand. It felt wrong to be the size that I was, but it was also right. I fell back onto my paws and tried to roll Asmoday again. I couldn't see him beneath me, but I felt the sting of his blade as he gained foot and retaliated.

Falling back, I uncoiled to get away from his slashes. Fire burst through the air as the demon's blade swung at my side. My scales protected me, but just barely. Moving backwards was much harder than going forward. I had a freakishly long middle and a tail to contend with. Asmoday laughed and sliced at me and finally, he broke through my fumbling attempts at dexterity. As I was trying to steady myself, the blade sliced along my tail.

"Back, Beast!" Asmoday laughed. That was rich. Although, to be fair, anyone watching this fight would have trouble telling the "bad" guy apart from the "good." My jaws snapped at him as he advanced. Tail swooshing out of the way of his blade, I saw red droplets fly into the air. My tail burned like hell, as if he'd grazed my thigh with a razor.

I was overthinking this. What would I do if I was in my human form? I was far from the strongest supernatural out there. What gave me an edge was quick thinking and precision. I'd parry him and go for his weakness. Which, as far as I could tell, were his animal heads and his hooved shorter leg. The sand between the toes of my claws was burning hot. My paws were my hands, I reminded myself. Back paws pushing into the sand, my head rose off the ground. My long neck followed it and my head with it. For a moment, it was out of Asmoday's reach. I swiped my claws at him-left to distract and right to grab his sword arm. My claws raked him across the torso, but he was ready for my attempt to disarm him. The pommel slammed into the soft tissue between my fingers-if that's what they were called now-and the thumb. Then, he twisted under my grasp and I heard something tear deep within my shoulder. This was when I realized that I'd ignored my greatest weapon. My jaws. Just as he was looking for a place to stab, I swung my head down and bit into his armpit.

I'd never bitten anyone before. The ram head bleated over my head and my mouth tasted like rotting copper.

It wasn't quite blood, but it wasn't the purple sludge that ran through devourers' veins either. Fire caught the edge of my vision. I felt a sting at my side as his sword sliced my scales. Through the pain, I released his side and bit into his satyr leg. Asmoday screamed and the fiery metal of the sword punched through my skin at the right shoulder. It hurt like a motherfucker. Screeching, I flung away from him.

As I rolled backwards, my body momentarily caught air. I felt my body move on instinct and felt my tail uncurl to catch balance. Okay, okay. I could figure this out.

Pushing off my back legs, I spiraled forward. This was a bit like being underwater. Only there was more gravity to contend with. My body was light and airy. As if in response to my daring, my scales flashed blue at the edges of my vision. For three blissful seconds, I was airborne. I crashed on top of Asmoday. My front paws slammed into his chest and my weight bore him down. We grappled with him quickly getting the better of me. I might've had the mass on my side, but he had the skill. Plus, he had centuries to get used to his fighting form. He was rapidly gaining advantage, and I followed an instinct I didn't know I had. He rolled me over and I let him. Then, I used his own force against him and coiled the length of my body around him. My right paw was seriously hurt, but I had the rest of my body to work with. For a second, the sword was thrust to the side and my paw was pressing it down. Slowly, my scaly body began crushing him. The ram head bleated and the bull head bellowed. Asmoday's humanoid face twisted. I felt a fleeting moment of triumph before my throat swelled.

Suddenly, I couldn't breathe. His blood burned its way down my gullet. I sprang back and heaved. My entire body recoiled, but nothing would come out.

Asmoday laughed and rose to his feet. He walked toward me. "You'll find the taste of my blood too strong for your tongue, Veles' spawn!" His limp was familiar now—his satyr leg was the same leg that we thought had taken a bullet in the line of ERS duty. How naïve we'd all been. Brandishing his sword, he charged me. "Let's give yours a taste."

He swung at my neck, and I fell backwards. It would've been nice if my translucent form was invincible, like Mittens'. Alas, I was solid and beheading was a very real threat. My right paw bucked as I fell to the side. The wound pulsed, and silvery blood spilled onto the ground. The thirsty sand of the devourer's desert soaked it right up. I snapped my jaw at his head, but he was ready this time. Elbowing me in the eye, his sword grazed my neck.

I felt unsteady and the blood in the back of my throat burned. All at once, I could feel myself with uncomfortable completeness. Every translucent muscle and every scale and every suddenly clumsy paw. I shook my head to clear the cobwebs. Asmoday grinned. His demonic jaw unhinged as he did, and the corners of his mouth drew back unnaturally far. He was so huge now that the glowing fireflies of the souls danced in and out of his grinning maw. Swelling again, his spine popped and his sword flared brighter. He wasn't shy about eating the souls now. And why not? It's not like he had the Gates of Hell to break down. The only thing he had to break now was me.

Swinging the sword with confidence and skill, he began backing me into a devourer's nest.

I knew what he was doing, and I seriously, *seriously* didn't want to get trapped in there. I wasn't used to fighting on land, or fighting in my dragon form at all. Worse, my body wasn't listening to me. Something was seriously wrong with my movement control. I pushed back on my front legs as Asmoday's sword swooshed past my chest. Springing off my back coils, I sank my teeth into the bull's head. The Prince of Hell bashed my temple with his pummel. Rearing back, I released the bull and shook out my head. I was feeling all sorts of weird. Outside of having a twenty-foot body and a tail.

"I warned you," he said. "Tasting my blood isn't all it's cracked up to be." His heads doubled in my vision as I felt my back paws scrape down an opening in the sand. Familiar paralysis began in my back legs. Oh no, not *again*. Asmoday was poison, and I'd just taken a serious bite out of him. At least his limp was more of a hobble now, and the bull's head hung limply off his shoulder. Despite it, his grin didn't falter. What did it matter if he had thousands of lives to burn through? The blue flared in his mouth and the bull's head perked up. My back paws were unfeeling as they slid into the nest. Bones crunched under the weight of my body, and the stench of whatever prey devourers killed in Hell rose around me.

Swinging from the shoulder, Asmoday's massive arms drove the sword into my chest.

25

I THINK WHAT SAVED me was that he couldn't find my heart. Shit, I wasn't even sure where it was. The sword burned as it stabbed through my ribs and into whatever anatomical goodies lay beneath. I howled in pain. It came out like the cry of a wounded animal, which, at the moment, I was.

"You ruined years of planning," Asmoday's voice came down on my head. "A perfect opportunity, wasted. If you think you can just go to your daddy's realm, you are sorely mistaken. I will personally drain you. Your soul will never see rebirth. I hope it was worth it."

The blood filling my mouth was now my own. I sank into the bones below and my eyes fluttered closed. There was a noise somewhere in the distance, something like babies crying through phone static. Darkness was a warm, sticky wave that pulled me under. My body uncoiled as my muscles spasmed. Every cell in my body was pain. Wasn't poison supposed to make you feel good before you died? Maybe I was thinking of drugs. That I'd technically won was no longer making me feel any better. Dying in a filthy devourer pit and having my soul turned into a husk by a Prince of Demons? Astrid would laugh. It was no more than a soul eater like me deserved. The static slithered through my awareness again. This time, it was closer. It was like a bee in my ear, refusing to let me slip into the abyss. I wasn't sure I liked that. There was release in the abyss. No more pain. No more uncertainty of whether I was a monster. Just an ERS rescuer dying in the line of duty.

My eyes opened as Asmoday wrenched out his sword. The pain was distant now, but the blood was immediate. It poured out of my chest like quicksilver. I was lying on my back in a pile of filth. The stench that came from under me was unbearable. He raised his sword and his slitted eyes searched my scales. He snarled a grin. My heart thudded. I knew without a doubt that his next stab wouldn't miss it.

Take them.

The dragon's voice—*my* voice cut through the pain. The static was so loud in my ears, I couldn't hear my own raggedy breath. Wailing cries filled my awareness.

Take them home.

I knew where the cries were coming from. It was the souls wailing inside Asmoday. A shepherd, that's what he'd called me. Tick's words came to mind as I watched the sword descend in slow motion.

"You can't blame someone's nature. Gotta trust it, you know?"

My song spilled out into my mind. I didn't need lips to sing it, and the words could've been sung in any language at all. My dragon's song. *My* song. Veles was the god of cattle and the god of the dead. It was no wonder it was the tunes of the shepherds that had struck a literal chord inside me. I was not a Soul Devourer. Those five souls in Hades weren't taken for keeps, but to take them back to where they belonged. I was a Soul Shepherd, and I would take these souls home. Asmoday's sword was an inch from my collar bones that hid the beating of my heart.

"Small goat, little goat, come to my stead. Not where, not there, but here instead. I will groom you, I will feed you, tie you to a stake. Come to me, to my stead, not there but here instead."

Asmoday bucked. It looked like someone had punched him in the solar plexus. His humanoid eyes widened. The ram's head bleated. It was a low, horrible sound. The bull's head rolled its horns, eyes bulging. The flame of his sword flicked out.

"What—" He gasped. "What are you doing?"

Like your soul being yanked out, is what Tick had said about my power. Asmoday didn't have a soul. All he could do was power himself by eating others'.

Spirits *leaked* out of him. I don't know what I'd expected, but it wasn't blue, sooty light escaping the folds of his skin, his nostrils, and his mouth. His eyes flicked from red to blue as lights spilled out of them. They drifted toward my maw. I inhaled every single one. They were *amazing*. Filling me with air and light, each life that passed between my teeth settled into my tummy.

"Stop it!" Asmoday wailed. "Stop!"

He choked and gagged on the familiar fireflies. Water Babies. Children's laughter filled the air, and I welcomed them in. I welcomed them *all*. The Paiute babies and the souls I'd failed to save with my ERS van. There were others, too. Souls he'd stored but hadn't used in his time on Earth. There weren't many, but they flashed in my mind just the same. Hopes and dreams. Lives lived and laughter laughed. Agony and violence, too. There couldn't be light without darkness. I drew them in and Asmoday shrank. His two animal heads disappeared, and he was back to resembling Chief Baran. The face of my boss looked down at me. There was no murder in his eyes anymore. Instead, there was panic.

"Green—" he choked out. "How—"

Each soul took a bit of Asmoday with him. Soon, the only thing that stood over me was just who I'd summoned when I was twelve. His hands were circled around his throat as if he was trying to contain whatever spirits were still inside. I looked up at him against the bloody sky. My teeth still tasted of blood—mine and his—but the contentment that settled over me was bliss. Souls swarmed in my belly. I couldn't use them to heal or to grow stronger. That's not what they were *for*. They were my charges, my herd. My responsibility. And he would have to cut through my belly to get to them.

Asmoday looked like he had other things to worry about. His human face was no longer handsome. Succubus blood had failed him, as there were no more souls to feed his life. Or whatever one could call life in his case. He was ashen and his teeth were yellow as he bared them at me.

"Mercy," he said. His voice was hoarse. "Please."

Lizzy's face flashed in my vision. She'd never got the chance to beg. The souls were buzzing inside me. Safe and sound. He would've drained each one.

There wasn't a doubt in my mind that what he was feeling was horrible. I was a rescuer, and I often saved those who didn't deserve it. But my *mercy* had its limits.

I sang until his body stooped with old age. I sang until his body began to crumble and still I sang. I didn't stop until every last one of the souls he'd stolen was gone.

His form swayed in the scorching wind of Hell. It collapsed like an empty hornet's nest and his husk fluttered on the bones of devourers' victims. Asmoday was gone. The souls were safe.

The breeze caressed my scales and I could no longer smell the stench. My blood was leaving me with every beat of my dragon's heart. Inch by inch, I began crawling out of the nest. I couldn't imagine how I could survive this, but I couldn't lie in the pile of bones and die. Those souls had trusted me. They came to me when I called. I owed them more than that.

My human self emerged from under my scales as I made my way out of the nest and onto the orange sand. Immediately, I wondered if that was wise. There is no sun in Hell, but the heat beats down just the same. Without my dragon form, I lay naked under the brick-red sky. Asmoday might've missed my heart, but he'd stabbed me somewhere bad. There was wheezing in my breaths. Black dots stabbed my vision. My blood was no longer silver but honest-to-gods human red. The sand washed over me as the wind picked up speed.

Rolling over, I curled around the wound in my chest. I pressed a fist to the puncture. It was narrower on my human body than it had been on my shifter form. Small mercies.

I imagined myself—a small dot in the middle of a devourer desert. Would its owners come back and find an easy meal? My palm pressed into my stomach. I could feel the souls hum a satisfied hymn. I wasn't just one life right now; I was thousands. Teeth gritted, I crawled. Somewhere in the red sand was the Crystallizer. It didn't have a surge, but it had metal walls. I could wait there for rescue. Or death.

I don't remember at which point I blacked out. Even a demigoddess could only take so much. My body's battery simply ran out on me. I remember wondering if the sky was falling down, and then a pair of hands were shaking me.

"Chrys," a man's voice appeared in my consciousness. "For gods' sake, wake up."

I was lying half buried in the sand. Like that time my mom and I dug ourselves into the beach of Lake Tahoe and made mermaid tails. Funny.

"Please, Chrysoberyl."

Muttered curses and pleas in Old Slav followed. I opened my eyes and saw Zan's dimpled chin and pale gray eyes. His chest deflated in relief when he saw me stir.

"Oh, Chrys-" His hand cupped the back of my head. "Oh, baby. Why did you have to go after him when you knew you couldn't get out?"

His other hand sliding under my knees, he lifted me out of the sand. The way he was handling me I might as well have been a Fabergé egg. I wanted to laugh, but my breath wouldn't cooperate. Ugly bubbling came from my chest.

"Hush," he said. "I got you."

He cradled me in his arms. I could smell rain and tawny feathers and the aftermath of battle. He smelled like Zan. That beat the shit out of the smell of a devourer's nest.

"The— the treaty," I managed. "You can't be here."

His smile was faint, but his hand was reassuring as he stroked my hair.

"Don't you know this already? I'd go to war for you, Veles' daughter."

Did he actually say that? It didn't seem quite right and I couldn't trust myself to know for sure. The swaying sent my consciousness crawling back into the recess of my mind. Last thing I saw was eagle feathers sprouting out of Zan's shoulders.

26

Threatening to lick my boots, waves teased the rocky shore. Wind picked up my hair as I looked across the Pyramid Lake. The early morning sun was just warming my head. Goosebumps covered my arms. I made the drive right before sunrise to avoid the boats and the prying eyes. Breathing a lungful of air, I winced. Pain shot through the left side of my chest. The shallower cuts that Asmoday had dealt me had healed within a week. But the deep stab had pierced my left lung and my liver. When Zan dragged me out of Hell, I was in terrible shape. Heal Hands had brought me back from the brink of death. As a matter of fact, Henry would berate me for being here. I was supposed to be on bed rest for another two days. Smiling, I rolled my shoulders. It felt good to be out in the fresh air. The water smelled like weeds and stone. Although, I had to admit that playing video games with Rudy while I recovered wasn't the worst thing in the world. The only downside was having to scrape frost off my controller whenever he lost at Mario Kart. At least he'd stopped glaring at me for ditching him at the Gates. My apartment door was officially no longer a vaulted door. Mittens was stoked to have another lap to scratch. Not that, much to my mom's disappointment, I'd finally "nailed down a guy." Having a friend—and not just a coworker—was a good enough start for me.

Anticipation rolled through me. I'd been waiting for this day for weeks. Throwing a glance over my shoulder, I stripped off my clothes. I wasn't worried about someone seeing my naked ass, of course. My shifter form would be much more of a shocker.

As if sensing their closeness to the Lake, the Water Babies hummed in my belly. I gave it a brief run as my ankles broke the cold water. Soon, my limbs were claws and my skin was scales. I wasn't cold anymore as I became my dragon.

The water split before me as I swam. My skin tingled with pleasure. It'd been years since I'd been bold enough to swim in open water. I wasn't a monster and I wasn't afraid. Not anymore. My shifter form had a purpose. *I* had a purpose. And I was here at the Lake to fulfill it. I serpentined through a terrified school of fish. My claws raked and curled up into my body as I crossed the length of the water between the shore and Anaho Island. I pushed upward, and my head resurfaced in the morning mist.

I used the rising sun to my advantage. If someone saw my translucent, horned head poking out of the water, they'd take it for a mirage. I let the warmer surface water hold my body in its embrace. Everything was still and if I closed my eyes, I could no longer separate myself from the nature around me. We vibrated on the same frequency.

Pointing my gaze to the sky, I opened my jaw.

Your shepherd has brought you home, I thought to the souls collected between my coils. *You are free.*

A pressure inside me pushed out and up. There was that laughter again, the kind that broke over the surface of the water like falling rain. Joy and hope. Future. In the morning light, they were barely perceptible. Thousands of sparks dotted the space over my head. Piercing through the last of the mist, the sun caught them and made them flare. They were *so* beautiful. Each one a life ready for another chance. The air carried them like dandelion seeds as they drifted toward the sky and disappeared into the blue.

I stayed there for as long as I dared. Human or dragon, my body was still weak. I felt lighter, though, and a little *lonely.* I hoped that whatever Underworld those babies had chosen, it would be kinder to them than the human world.

Next stop for me would be Hades. As soon as Stonefield got clearance, I would return the five souls I'd taken two years ago. I was now officially a soul taxi. Beat the shit out of the "Devourer."

Back on the shore, I pulled on my clothes. I raked my hands through my wet hair and piled it into a bun at the top of my head. I checked my phone and saw that I had a missed called from Jaro. Frowning, I pressed the screen to call him back.

"What's up, Green?" the son of Perun said into the phone. His usually cheerful tone carried a note of worry. "You all done purging the goods?"

I smiled. "That's one way to put it." Licking my lips, I tried not to sound too eager as I asked. "Have you heard from him?"

It was as if I could see Jaro shaking his head. "Nope. The domovois sent another message to our father's house. The only reply we got is that Zan's 'busy.' Whatever the hell that means."

Shaking my head, I kicked a stone. "How much trouble is he in? Really?"

The twins were scarce with the details while I was lying on my deathbed. Soon after he'd brought me back, Zan was summoned to Perun's hold in Prav—the godly plane of Vyraj. It had to do with him going to Hell to save me, of course. He was his father's heir, and a famed demon slayer. His actions broke the Spiral's pact of nonaggression between the pantheons. If he wanted to, Lucifer could interpret Zan's interference in his realm's business as an act of war.

"Honestly?" Jaro said. "We don't know. Dad's never been good at handling rebellious shit."

"I'm sure that me being Veles' daughter doesn't help," I said.

"Probably not," he admitted.

"Okay," I said. "Thanks for letting me know. Keep me posted?"

"Bet."

Jaro hung up the phone, and I stared at it for a few long seconds. I wasn't sure that I'd heard what I thought I'd heard in the devourer nest. It had sounded a lot like Zan confessing that he was still carrying a torch for me.

I snorted. As if. My heart beat just thinking about it, though. That wasn't right. I focused on being thankful. If he hadn't come for me, I'd be dead and all the souls I'd been carrying would be trapped in Hell. This lead me to another thought that'd been bothering me of late. What did Asmoday mean about a "few short years" at the Gate? What would happen?

"Be okay, Zan," I whispered. His dad was mad at him, but it wasn't like the Spiral had opened a case against him. That couldn't be all that bad, right?

Walking uphill, I smiled at the sight of Crystallizer parked on the side of the road. It had been polished to a shine. The bright purple was vivid and the mushrooms on the sides looked like I'd painted them yesterday. Once everything came to light, Director Stonefield appointed a new van to Rudy and me. I hadn't been inside it. Right now, I had *my* van. Personally pulled from Hell by Uncle Ophis, and smelling of incense and weed.

Looking bored, Tick leaned out of the passenger window. Their freshly colored orange hair fell into their eyes as they rolled them.

"Took you long enough, Dragon Princess." They tapped the wheel. Handy waved at me over their shoulder. "We're late for our trippy road trip. I got things to smuggle and debts to repay." Their smile was sharp as they jingled the keys. "Can I drive?"

I reached out my hand and answered with a grin of my own. "Absolutely not."

THE END

About the Author

Elena Sobol is many things, but she's definitely—definitely—not five pigeons wearing a trench coat. She lives in Utah with her husband, son, and a very spoiled cat.

To keep up with her shenanigans, visit:
www.elenasobol.net.

Or use the QR code below to sign up for her newsletter to receive updates on new books, art, and life.

Printed in Great Britain
by Amazon